THE LIGHT AND THE FAIR WORD
CAROLINE LOPEZ

THE LIGHT AND THE FAIR WORD

Table of Contents

CHAPTER 1
Bright Star

The blue and silver banners fluttered over the pinnacles of the castle, but it was impossible to see them from inside the dungeon.

It was hard to see much of the outside world at all from within those wide, windowless rooms that had been built into the great rock on which the castle called Prisma stood. But at least the dungeon wasn't actually underground. That would have been worse. And it would have been harder to get the horses in and out of it that way.

King Nereus was both fair and prosperous enough to keep more horses than he did captives, and had converted the disused dungeon into stalls and pens for these horses, a mew for the carriages they pulled, and barracks for the stablehands who tended them. He felt it was a better use of the space to house his animals and their grooms, than to hold any enemies of the kingdom of Ausonia.

But despite the lack of imprisonment or torture, the scarcity of sunlight in the place still lent it an oppressive atmosphere, and so the great wooden doors were often thrown open to let in light and air, and allow the stablehands a view of the great green field called Palomba, which surrounded the castle.

Though sometimes more than just these things came in through the doors.

Dario, the head groom, discovered this when he spied the shadow of someone much too small to be one of his workers moving behind the post where Prince Vanya's prized white hunting horse waited for its rider.

"What do you think you're doing back there, son?" Dario growled, pulling the young intruder out by his collar. "Don't you know whose horse this is, or for that matter, whose home this is? You can't just come into the king's castle uninvited."

"I was only looking."

The excuse was not given meekly, but as a matter of fact, with shades of what Dario might even call annoyance, as if Dario were the one bothering *him*.

He shook the boy, preparing to rebuke him again, but another voice interrupted him.

"What a cute little stableboy. Is he new?"

This was the voice of Prince Vanya, sauntering in with riding crop in hand and a smile on his face, dressed in the same silver and blue as the banners which blew over the high roofs of the castle above them.

"He's no cute little boy," answered Dario. "He was sneaking around on your property like a thief."

"I was not!" was the response, in a tone that Dario had heard courtiers use when their reputations had been called into question. It wasn't fitting for a child to speak to adult that way, and Dario said as much to the prince, who only laughed at both of them, with a sound like moving water.

Vanya knelt down before the boy. "Can you tell me what you were doing?"

"I just wanted to see the horses. I wasn't going to do anything to them, and I wasn't going to steal."

"I like horses, too," Vanya smiled. "Did you know that people like Dario get to work with them all the time? Isn't that wonderful? I wish I could do it for my job."

"Job?" As the prince had intended, the child's anger was doused as quickly as it had flared, being replaced by sudden curiosity.

"Oh, yes," he said. "You even get paid for it."

"Could *I* do it?"

"Why not?"

Dario made a skeptical noise. "He's a bit young yet. How old are you, boy?"

"I could do it right now! I'm eight years old this month," the boy answered, chin raised.

Vanya, noting it, placed a hand on his own chest and bowed his head.

"I apologize for Dario's inhospitality, master, uh – how should I address my lord?"

"He means your name, son," Dario prompted when the child didn't respond. "What is it?"

"It's Euphemio."

"What's a boy destined to be a stablehand doing with such a name? A fancy name like that ought to belong to someone of quality, not a person who'll be mucking out horse stalls all their days."

"You can call me Euphy if it's too hard for you," the young eyes flashed as he said it, until Vanya interrupted them again.

"Just because someone isn't born to privilege doesn't mean they aren't worthy of respect. If my opinion is worth anything, my lord Euphemio," he said, looking down at the young face. "I think you have great potential to become someone of quality, and I'm honored that you want to work in our stable. I trust that our horses will be well taken care of in your hands."

Then, to Dario, he added "I trust you'll take care of our new employee."

"What, you really mean right now?" Dario sputtered.

Vanya simply grinned at him, and climbed lightly onto the back of his waiting white horse.

"He can do it. It wasn't so long ago that I was his age."

"Only sixteen years! Not long at all!"

"It doesn't feel like a long time to me," Vanya shrugged, and turned to address Dario's new charge.

"Now, Euphemio, can you untie those reins you see looped around the post there?"

Euphy scrambled forward to perform his first official duty, his small hands easily untying the knots.

"See?" said Vanya to Dario, then clicked his tongue at his mount, who cantered gaily through the open doors, and Euphy watched in awe as horse and rider shot forward once they reached sunlight, out onto Palomba Meadow. The horse's mane flew like another banner in the wind, and the prince's hand was as light on the reins as if that wind was the only thing directing their course.

But Euphy's admiration of the sight was interrupted by a shovel, too large for him by half, being pushed into his own hand.

"I guess you've gotten yourself hired. Congratulations. Now you get to find out what it means to *earn* your living," Dario informed him.

"I can't use something this big."

"You're the one who said you could work here. Don't tell me you've changed your mind."

Euphy looked back through the doors, at the white horse shooting like a midday star over the wide green expanse, and the bright, joyful prince who had treated him like an equal, who had believed his words, and cheerfully stood up for him in the face of untruth. If working here meant being in the presence of someone like that, and having them on his side, then it would be worth what he'd have to deal with in exchange.

"I haven't changed my mind," he said.

He would remember those words when what was called the New Glory arrived, and the bright star disappeared into the night.

CHAPTER 2
Night of New Glory

It was everything out of a fairy tale and at the same time, nothing like one at all.

This was not how Euphy thought of the Night of New Glory. There had been no beauty in that, when the country awoke on a sunny morning three months into Euphy's new employment, to find that the king of blue and silver had been murdered while they slept, and his fine prince along with him, replaced by a new king with Albion blood, who, not ranking high enough amongst the nobility of that neighboring country to have any serious claim to its throne, had decided to claim the throne of another country by force.

There was nothing glorious about how the servants and castle staff, too lowly to be involved in politics, and too poor to refuse when the new king's men offered to let them keep their positions as long as they swore loyalty to their new ruler, took the offer in exchange for their honor.

Euphy hadn't understood the full consequences of these events until the night many years later, when he was drawn into the dark, strange fairy tale which surrounded King Livio the Iron Hand. On that night, Euphy was four years past the age that Vanya had been when they'd met, and he'd come to understand what the prince had meant when he said that sixteen years didn't feel like long ago at all.

It had been twenty years between that declaration and the night on which Euphy was woken by a trumpeting in the darkness. He stumbled out into the stone corridor that led from the grooms' narrow quarters to the wide wooden doors that the prince had passed through long ago. But the light that burst in through them when they were opened was even more brilliant than the light which had gone out of it on that day.

It was so bright that Euphy could barely see its source. But what he thought he saw was almost impossible to believe.

"Dario?" he asked, sure that the man who rarely missed an opportunity to correct him would set him right. "Is that really a…unicorn?"

The king's hunters – wild men who were hardly more human than the animals they pursued – yanked the white shape forward with chains as thick as anchor lines, while others prodded it from behind with spears like ship masts.

Euphy would've imagined that unicorns were delicate and dainty. But this animal was huge, as big as any draft horse, and Euphy felt the ground shaking as the creature blasted out its indignant call.

Its hooves were steel, or at least they shone like it, and they struck sparks against the rough stone floor as it walked. The only thing about the unicorn that looked like what Euphy had heard was the spiralled horn piercing the air as it furiously tossed its head.

How long had he stood there watching it? It already felt like hours by the time Dario, wary of the hunters who were beginning to scowl at the onlookers, smacked him on the arm.

"Go back to bed. I'll find out what's going on here, and I don't want you underfoot when I'm dealing with them."

Euphy doubted he'd get any sleep with the unicorn still trumpeting wildly, but he went back to his little room and laid down anyway.

When he closed his eyes, the darkness behind them was still punctuated by a blinding white light.

CHAPTER 3
Lady in the Tower

"Lord Stillshire, how was your tour of the Crescent Belt? What news do you have for me about our dear people from elsewhere in the country?" the king asked of the man across the council table in the Emerald Room.

"There are the usual grumblings from those who would throw you out if they could, but aside from that, there is nothing out of the ordinary."

"It's more than the ordinary," the councilman beside him cut in. "For whatever reason, the Ausonians are restless these days. Maybe it's because of the anniversary; this year makes twenty years."

"There have always been some who've never moved past the old days. That's nothing new," Stillshire objected.

"Why do we need to pretend like it isn't happening? This is why we've been trying to get the unicorn these days, isn't it?"

"Then let's give thanks that the unicorn has come to us just at this hour," the king said. "So that it can help me show them the right way of thinking."

"You could have done that anyway," said Stillshire earnestly. "You didn't need a unicorn when you brought the New Glory."

"But we should ensure that we don't live in the past, without continually improving ourselves and our strength. My predecessor failed to do so, and we know what his fate was, " Livio explained.

"Think of how much *more* glorious His Highness will be when he discovers how to borrow the unicorn's power," Sir Greycove spoke from down the table.

"We don't need to control it. Just take what we need from it," Lord Kerlin added his voice to the discussion. "Can't we just kill it?"

"How much power have you ever seen in a dead animal?" Stillshire returned.

More voices around the table were raised to give their opinions until the king, at the table's head, lifted his hand to silence them.

"I'm grateful that so many of you are concerned about me, and I appreciate you trying to help me, but I won't have any of my guests treated poorly. We will treat the unicorn with hospitality until it's ready to share its gifts."

"We could *make* it be ready faster if we went down there and – " Lord Kerlin started, but Livio cut the suggestion off with a sudden brusqueness that stopped every other voice.

"None of you are to enter its space. Is that understood?

No one spoke, but everyone agreed, and when Livio spoke next, it was again with a mildness that better suited someone who had not earned the name Iron Hand by laying waste to an entire monarchy overnight.

"I myself will keep a respectful distance from it, and what will it think of me if I don't ensure others do the same? It will think I'm someone not worthy of sharing anything with, if I fail to control my own subordinates."

The wary silence remained, and Livio, as if trying to erase the unpleasantness in the air, changed the subject by turning to the man who sat at his right hand.

"Tell me, Dandy. How is our other esteemed guest doing these days?"

"No trouble from that quarter, as usual."

"No trouble," the king repeated, sighing. "It's always the same."

"Isn't that what we want?"

"But I get so bored hearing it. Don't you miss the days when we had some new challenge to face every day?"

"Those were also the days before you became king."

"But at least they were interesting. I wish she would cause a fuss once in a while, just for something different. If she were rowdy like the rest of her people – if I had to use the unicorn's power to put her in her place, that could be diverting."

"I don't think she could put up a fuss even if she tried."

Dandy struggled to put on the dutiful smile he knew was expected of him. The idea of Livio using physical force on Theodora put a knot in his stomach. The possibility had always been there, but after twenty years of Livio allowing him to handle the business of the Nereus's daughter without interference, it was a possibility he'd grown used to ignoring.

"Don't look so serious. You know I'm joking," Livio said, watching Dandy's face fall.

The others around the table apparently found it easier to laugh along with him than Dandy did.

"You could've made a little effort to pretend," Lord Kerlin told him later. "You're smart enough to know that you've only gotten away with keeping her at all is because you toe the line in everything else. Just because you were friends with Livio before Ausonia doesn't mean you don't still have to respect him, even when you disagree with him.

Do you really want to lose everything you've worked towards so you can pine over some feather-headed woman who doesn't know you from a housecat?"

"Stop," said Dandy, with a firmer voice than he had used with the king.

"You'd better watch it, or you might get transferred to watching over the other guest. By the way, have you seen it? The unicorn?"

"I haven't. Not even Livio himself has been down there yet."

"I don't have to remind you not to bring your kept woman to look at it, do I?"

"To whom do you think you're speaking?" Dandy demanded. "Livio may be free to make such jokes to me, but *you* are not. Remember your place, Kerlin."

Theodora was still technically an enemy of the crown, and taking an enemy into the presence of the unicorn – which Livio was counting on to cement his power beyond the level which any human could promise – that was something Dandy would not be foolish enough to do.

Yet even if he were free to do it, he would not take her anywhere near a creature that had taken ten hardened hunters to capture. If it could outmatch that many of them for strength, what could it do to a woman who didn't even remember that the castle she lived in was no longer her own, and that people around her now were the same ones who had murdered her family in the night?

Aside from anything to do with the unicorn, a new dread began to grow as Dandy climbed the stairs, leaving Kerlin behind and crossing the corridors that led to Theodora's rooms. He hated that every time he saw her, he had to wonder how much more of herself she'd lost since the last time, or which version of her he would find today.

Dandy had seen battles in his day, and looked in the face of many enemies. But recently, the two things he feared the most were:

One: That Theodora would forget everything at last, and he would come to visit her only to find she did not recognize him at all.

Two: That she would remember everything instead, and he would come to visit her only to find that she hated him.

When he knocked on her door in his usual way (for despite what Lord Kerlin might think, they did *not* have any sort of improper relationship), he was shown in by Marta, the lady's maid, with Theodora soon appearing behind her. Her spangled silks swished gently as she moved to take Dandy's hands.

"I've been waiting for you to get here," she said. "How was your meeting?"

This was promising. She remembered what he'd told her about his schedule this morning. But he hesitated to answer. The unsettling turn the discussions surrounding her had taken wasn't something he wanted to repeat.

"Let's not talk about it," he said, and turned his attention to a small, framed, portrait sitting on the mantle above Theodora's fireplace. The painting showed a prince in blue and silver, on a white horse with a green field behind him, looking as if he were trying to put on a serious face, but whose smile was creeping into the edges of his mouth, and into the sparkling eyes which were greener than the grass.

If Livio knew it was here, he would not have allowed it. But he would never find it out from Dandy.

"That's my brother," said Theodora. She was telling Dandy what he already knew, but he was no less glad to hear it.

"His name meant something lovely in an old language."

Now this was something new, something she'd never told him before.

"Which old language?"

"Hmm?"

"Your brother's name. It meant something in some foreign language?"

"Oh? And what did it mean, Dandy? Something nice?"

Dandy couldn't hold her innocently questioning gaze, knowing that she had slipped away from him again. These little glimpses of her old life, her old self, found their way back once in a while, but they were often gone as fast as they had come.

At this point, Dandy probably knew more about her past than she did herself, and even what he knew wasn't much.

She had been a princess in this castle years ago, before the New Glory. But had she always been this way? Barely aware of what was happening around her, much less who and what she had been before the Albionite army, with Dandy at its head, had marched on her home and claimed the kingdom for Livio?

He sometimes considered it a miracle that she even recognized him from day to day. Somehow, even after these years in which she forgot more and more about her own life, she was always able to recall him, who served as ambassador between the king and the last heir of Nereus. He'd been the one to convince Livio that holding Theodora captive under his power would be the final, most painful blow to the honor of her family, while at the same time, she could pose no real threat to Livio's authority if she couldn't even remember that she had a right to.

"My brother's name was Vanya," she was saying. "What did it mean, Dandy?"

"I can't tell you. I don't know."

"I wish you could have met him. And I wish I could remember more about him."

But Dandy *had* met Prince Vanya, and he certainly remembered him. How could he forget the prince he had killed?

CHAPTER 4
Once By Your Name

"If Livio wanted his carriage horses today, he shouldn't have brought that creature in to spook them. They won't work when they're spooked," the unmistakably gruff voice of Dario could be heard complaining.

"Don't you know anything?" returned Stregatto, the hunter who had come to deliver Livio's request. "Unicorns are supposed to have magic and power, and that sort of thing's useful to a king."

"The old king didn't need such things to make him great."

"And where is the old king now?" asked Stregatto.

Dario turned away. When it came down to it, who was to say that one of these men hadn't been there, hadn't done it themselves, when Nereus had been murdered? Dario might not have minded blustering against those who couldn't fight back, but he knew he was out of his depth with the hunters.

They were feral and savage beyond the ordinary level of the intruders who had brought so much destruction from Albion. They had to be, in order to capture a creature of the unicorn's enormous size and ferocity.

The hunters under Nereus used to bring in deer and such things as were necessary to feed the castle's inhabitants, but these strange, wild men had brought in a strange, wild animal, and the servants were left to deal with the consequences, the same as they had been on the first morning of the New Glory.

13

Dario muttered under his breath all the way until he reached Euphy, and told him, "I've got to get the carriage hacks ready, which means you're on creature duty."

He jerked his thumb over his shoulder to the pen that was normally used for the wildest of horses – those that would kick down a wooden stall door – until they could be trained to accept a harness or saddle.

The walls enclosing the pen were more than twice as tall as Euphy, and were made of stone which no horse could kick down, while a metal gate formed of heavy iron bars served as the entrance. It had previously been used as a solitary confinement space when this had been a dungeon for human prisoners, but now it housed the captive unicorn.

Rings which had once held the chains of men, but which now held the chains of the creature, were bolted to the walls, and cuffs that could fit around a man's thigh were needed to enclose the unicorn's feathery pasterns.

"What am I supposed to do with it?" Euphy asked, not eager to have to come face to face with what was behind those walls.

"The same as you do with all the others. Just feed it, water it, muck out the pen, and there you go. I don't need to tell you not to bother it while you're in there, do I?"

"No, you don't," said Euphy, and meant it. He'd dealt with horses near that size before. Draft horses meant for hard labor could be as big as that, or near it, but for however imposing they looked, they were at least docile. Someone in the far past had had the foresight to breed cold blood and calm temperaments into them to balance out their strength.

But this creature, if the confused images of the night before were anything to go by, had fire to match every bit of its size, and Euphy would rather not risk aggravating something so dangerous. Beautiful, but dangerous all the same. He felt terrible thinking it, but he was glad, just at this moment, that the thing was chained.

14

As he gathered his supplies, he repeated to himself that he would simply get in, do what he had to do, and get out. He might stay unscathed if he did not look at it, prod it, or disturb it in any way.

He didn't expect to have to include speaking to it in that list.

He heard the voice as soon as he entered the pen, a voice impossible to mistake for one of the hunters, or Dario, or anyone else he had ever known.

It was the sound of fire crackling, and of metal striking metal.

"Human," the creature said.

The single word made Euphy jump, the bucket he carried splashing water onto his feet.

"Um...?" Euphy said. He'd been determined to do his job quietly, but he could no more refuse to answer than he could refuse an avalanche coming down a mountain. It would exact something from him whether he acknowledged it or not. He felt that the voice had already taken something from him. Or perhaps given it to him. He wasn't sure which.

"Release me," it commanded.

Euphy shook his head. The unicorn may have enchanted his voice out of him, but he could still control his own actions. If he did something so stupid as to try and free it, either the unicorn would gore him, the king would have his head, or both.

"It's not my business," he mumbled. "And besides, I don't have the key. Not to those chains anyway," he added, noting how the unicorn looked pointedly at the ring of keys on his belt. It was odd how it could give such a human look with its shining, otherworldly eyes.

But it didn't speak any more, and he avoided its gaze for the remainder of his time in the pen. When he slunk back out of the gate, he had to remind himself to stand up straight, that he hadn't done anything wrong. He'd followed his orders exactly. But hearing the angry stamps and the rattle

15

of chains in the padlocked pen made him feel worse than anything Dario or the hunters could have done to him if he had.

He told no one of the exchange afterward, and the unicorn didn't address him again, though it reared at him as best it could every day for two weeks when he came to care for it, and Euphy became adept at dancing around its silver hooves.

After two weeks, it stopped attempting to rear at him. After three weeks, it was not even standing. It lay on the ground most of the time, ate little, and its pale hide glowed a little less each day, to the point where it was beginning to look decidedly grey.

For all that it was a magical creature, Euphy knew enough to recognize sick animal when he saw one. Even the humblest wild thing hated being held captive, and this was no humble creature.

He felt bad enough for it, but what made it worse was knowing that the king would be displeased if the unicorn – the key to his dreams of greater power – died on Euphy's watch.

He needed to try something.

He thought of the bolt cutters that he used around the stable to repair things like broken gates or even do quick fixes on the undersides Livio's carriages when they needed repairs and there wasn't time to get them to the wainwright.

But these we made to do simple work on average metal. Chains which could hold a unicorn who was as big as a draft horse, and probably twice as strong even in poor health, could not be conquered by such small, weak instruments, whose blades wouldn't even fit around the width of one link.

No, tools wouldn't do. He would have to rely on his own wits if he wanted to make a difference.

"Are you...alright?" he finally managed to ask. For as much as he couldn't stop himself from speaking when a unicorn asked something of him, it was somehow equally difficult to break the silence imposed by one.

"It is not your concern," said the unicorn with its flickering-fire voice.

"Should I call someone to help you?" Euphy knew he sounded silly, especially because there was no one else he *could* call. He was the unicorn's groom. He ought to be one who knew how to care for it, but it was unthinkable that he should even touch the creature.

"Whom would you call?" it asked, as if reading his thoughts.

"The king?" Euphy tried. It was Livio who had wanted the unicorn. Let him deal with it, and get gored for his own trouble.

"If you bring him here, I will kill you both!" The fire flared hot, and the steel swords in the unicorn's voice clanged. It rose to its feet, but only briefly, then folded its huge, elegant legs underneath it and lowered itself again, panting for breath.

"If you're getting winded like that now, I doubt you'd be able to do much to the king," said Euphy, though it was difficult for him to catch his own breath after that.

He'd not said it to be unkind. Mostly, it was out of concern that this magnificent beast could have declined so much. But the unicorn's eyes that had glared at him a minute ago became so hurt and offended that Euphy regretted speaking at all.

"I'm sorry, unicorn. I didn't mean…" he said, but it didn't feel right to simply call the animal by what it was.

"Is there something else I can call you? Do you have a name?"

It didn't respond. The silence had settled again like a frost.

Euphy left determined not to make a mistake like that again. He would find a name to call it, even if he had to make one up himself. But he would not walk away from another of these conversations – if they could be called conversations – with the unicorn fading quietly behind him. He would do something to make it find its fire again.

17

He would not call it "beast" or "creature" for that was how the hunters called it. But what, then? How was he to pick a name for a unicorn?

None of the names he could think of sounded nice enough. Dario sometimes made fun of his name – "Euphemio" – for being too high-sounding. Perhaps that would have been a good choice if it hadn't been his own. He didn't think the unicorn would enjoy being named after the groom it hated, either.

He knew there was a library somewhere in the castle where information about almost any subject could be found for free, though he'd never been there. Maybe it would have some information about names. How to pick them, or what they meant.

Euphy could read – he'd been to school for a year or two before he'd started working – but the daily slog of trying to run a stable didn't leave him much time for recreation, and he preferred to spend the free time he did have in the nearby town of Clockface or anywhere away from Prisma.

But he was willing to try in this case, and he only hoped he wouldn't look too out of place amongst the scholars and clerics, or any of the other types of people who might frequent a library.

He had to make his way by following the directions on a scrap of paper given to him by one of the kitchen cooks, who sometimes went there to research Albion recipes, and when he reached the entrance, he looked up to find himself in a place that was so tall and airy he would not have guessed it was part of the same building as the dungeon stable.

He stood within a soaring atrium, flanked by rows upon rows of walkways on each side, rising to the ceiling, and each stacked high with shelves of neatly lined books. It was an impressive sight, but it's being so grand also meant that

Euphy had no idea where amongst the many shelves he ought to start searching.

He glanced around, trying not to look too obviously like someone unused to being here. After a minute, he noticed a desk which people sometimes approached and spoke to the intelligent-looking woman sitting behind it.

She appeared to be giving them instructions, or directions. Occasionally, she would write something on a piece of paper and hand it to them.

Taking a breath and reminding himself that this couldn't possibly be as hard as having to approach the unicorn, he stepped forward.

"Excuse me. Are there any books here about names?"

"Names?"

"What they mean. How to find out if a name means something in particular. Or how to choose the best name for someone?"

"You're looking for Onomastics?"

"Maybe? I guess so?"

"That would be in the Omega section."

It was only after he'd thanked her and turned away that Euphy realized he didn't know where the Omega section was, or how to get there. But if he went back to ask, he'd look like a fool.

"Guess I'll find it myself, then," he muttered.

After a long search during which he had plenty of time to change his mind about the atmosphere feeling light and airy, he finally and managed to locate Omega. It was not, as he expected on the same or even the adjacent floor to the Nu or Pi sections, but was for some reason he could not guess, two floors away.

When he reached the aisle with the plaque bearing the word "Onomastics", he avoided the eyes of the man who was already at the other end of it. Instead, he tried to focus on the titles on his own end: *Proceedings of the Fourth Onomastic Symposium...Toponymic Ono-mastics in*

19

Geographical   Appellation...Studies   in   Onomastic Stratification…it didn't take long to decide that none of these were anything that he could use.

He thumbed through one called *Selecting Significant Names,* but was disappointed to find that it mainly contained advice to new parents on how important it was to give their baby a meaningful name, without actually listing any good examples.

"I know all that already," he whispered at the pages, but not too loudly, for the other man had moved closer.

By the time Euphy decided that the next two books weren't for him, the stranger was within a few arm's lengths. At the last moment before he would have to either move or confront the man, Euphy's eye fell on the likely-looking title of *Classical Names from Legend and Antiquity*, and he attempted to reach for it, but was interrupted by the man speaking to him.

"Oh, were you planning to check that one out?"

"I – sorry. Check out?" Euphy asked, raising his eyes to see that the man cut a distinguished figure in a long grey coat that was piped with red around the cuffs and collar – the same colors as Euphy's uniform.

"You know, to take it with you?"

"Is that allowed?"

"Haven't you checked out a book before?"

"I haven't been to a library at all before," Euphy admitted.

"Is that so? Well, it's really very simple. All you have to do is take the book to the front desk, tell the librarian you want to borrow it, and she'll do the rest. Would you like me to show you how?"

"No," Euphy said, uneager to display his ignorance in front of more than one person today. "I mean, thanks," he added, becoming aware that he probably sounded rude. "But I'd rather not. I'll just leave it here."

He hesitated to remove his fingers from the silver letters embossed on the spine. But he would have to live without knowing whether this was the book he was looking for, because this person, whoever he was, would end up taking it with him, and how was Euphy meant to get it back after that?

"How about we make a deal?" offered the man. "If you don't check it out, then I won't, either. Then both of us can come here and read it any time we like. How's that? It would be better than one of us having to wait until the other is done with it, don't you think?"

"How would…how would I know when you're done with it? And how would I get it once you were?"

The man smiled. "You bring the books back here when you're done with them. Then other people can take them to read. Why don't you let me show you, in case you find one you do want to hold onto?"

He picked up *Toponymic Onomastics*. "Let's use this one as an example."

"I…alright," Euphy stammered. He was no better here than he was with the unicorn.

He followed as this man led him through the winding floors back to the front desk, explaining the whole process of "checking out and in" as if it were a battle strategy. It was a welcome relief after having just spent so long wandering among stacks that had nothing to do with Omega or onomastics.

When they reached the desk, Dandy passed the book to the woman and pulled a small rectangle of paper from his pocket.

"You don't need to show your card, sir," she said. "I know who you are."

"Humor me this time," he said, then turned to Euphy.

"The library card tells the staff your name and helps them keep track of who is using which book. It also helps them know where to find a book if it doesn't come back when it's supposed to."

Euphy peered at the card on the desk, and saw the name *Dandridge Morning* written there.

"If someone doesn't bring their book back, what does the library do?"

"They charge you a fine you, for one thing."

"What happens if you don't pay the fine?"

"We chain you up in the dungeon," the librarian joked, but Euphy didn't see much that was funny about it, given that there was a poor creature chained up there at this very moment.

Did she know about that, and if she did, would she have cared? Did anyone in this castle besides himself actually know or care about it?

"Is there anything else you'd like to know?" the man called Dandridge Morning asked him.

"No, I think I've learned enough for today," Euphy said, choosing not to voice any of the thoughts he'd just been entertaining. "Thank you, Mr. Morning."

"Oh, call me Dandy. Everyone does."

"I'm Euphy, by the way. Euphemio, really, but Euphy for short."

"I'm not sure that'll fit on a library card," commented the librarian.

"It's not any longer than my name, and you have no trouble with that," Dandy reasoned with her.

Euphy noticed that he didn't address the other reason why his name might be more troublesome than Dandy's.

"Euphemio" sounded Ausonian, to the point that even people like Dario poked fun at how like royalty it sounded, while "Dandridge" obviously had its roots in Albion.

For the first few years of Euphy's life, it wouldn't have been anything that anyone would have noted. There had been overlap between the two neighboring countries for years, enough that the originally distinct languages they'd spoken had long since merged into one. And especially this close to the border, transplants from one country to the other were not unusual.

One of the main differences that had remained between them was that they'd kept their distinct naming traditions, though Euphy knew a fair number of native Ausonians who bore Abionite names, often for no other reason than that their parents had liked the sound of them. Of course, most of these people had been born before the Night of New Glory.

After that night, Livio himself had claimed the issue of names as one of the justifications for his rule. His own name was Ausonian, he'd said, so did he not also have some connection to the country? Did he not have some right to love it enough to save it from the faults of the previous king?

Those Albionites who had come into the country following Livio's accession seemed to love their leader, name and all, yet they sometimes looked less kindly on the names of those who were tied to Ausonia by more concrete means.

"It isn't that I – " the woman started, but Dandy cut her off.

"As a matter of fact, let's sign him up for a card right now,"

He gave her a look that clearly communicated his expectation that she mind him, under which she shrank and took down Euphy's information, writing his full name in neat, even letters on a card which read:

Royal Library of Prisma
Class B: Reader
Name: Euphemio Benedetti

On the back was Livio's coat of arms. It was the same one that Euphy wore on his uniform every day. But it somehow felt like more of a mark of distinction now. It meant he had permission to come into this grand place and take anything he wanted out of it.

"You've helped me a lot, Dandy. Thank you."

Dandy nodded. "Time to get back to work? It's about that time for me as well. If there's anything else I can teach you, please let me know."

"How should I find you, if I do?"

"Why don't we meet in Omega again? I expect to see you keeping up your studies. What do you say to this time tomorrow?"

Euphy surprised himself by nodding. He hadn't expected to find anyone to talk to in the library, to say nothing of making plans to meet them again, but the way this Dandy had used his influence to help Euphy reminded him of the way Prince Vanya had once done the same for him.

That was the kind of person Euphy wanted to be for the unicorn. And now that he knew how to research what could help it, he was one step closer to his goal. So in a way, Dandy had helped the unicorn, too.

CHAPTER 5
Golden

The sign read Clockface Market, and Euphy navigated through it more easily than he did the library, for the market's lanes all radiated out from a central point, just like numbers on a clock, which was how the market had gotten its name.

Clockface had been here before Livio's time, and those vendors and customers who had been here just as long took pride in reminding everyone of that fact, especially the Albionites who both bought and sold in the market alongside them.

But for whatever competition the Clockface denizens felt toward each other, it was less important than the chance to make money off of each other, and so the atmosphere at Clockface remained as bustling and as lively as any other market, especially one which served a town at the foot of a royal residence – or a town as close to it as was possible.

The village which shared its name with the market lay on the perimeter of Palomba Meadow and its lights were often visible from the windows of the castle, in contrast to many of the other towns throughout Livio's kingdom, which offered little besides misery and poverty as their main attractions.

Euphy wandered out from among the aisles, back to the market entrance. There wasn't anything he really wanted to spend his small bit of money on unless someone here sold magic talismans to restore the health of legendary beasts.

To the side of the entrance and the arch which crossed over it, a small crowd had gathered to watch a troupe of dancers. It wasn't unusual for traveling groups of entertainers to come to the market for a few days before moving on to the next town, though these were some of the most ragged looking dancers Euphy had seen.

They were dressed all in black tatters, their faces painted with pitch, and each of them carried a staff as they skipped and twirled, weaving between each other in patterns that shifted in time to a driving drumbeat. At intervals, they would strike each other's staffs, yelling with each clack of the wood.

It looked almost like a battle, with how they swung and shouted, and unease crept over Euphy as he watched. This shouting and striking, and fierce faces in the deepening shadows, was reminiscent of another night, when other voices shouted in the dark, and other weapons, sharper than these, were wielded to more solemn effect before the morning rose on a new era.

Amongst this unsettling group, one man in particular drew his attention. Though he was dressed in black tatters like the rest, he carried his head so nobly that the feather on his hat bobbed like a knight's plume, and his black cloak looked as if it had once been something finer than the threadbare scraps which hung from the shoulders of the others. When Euphy kept his eye on this man, he stopped feeling quite so bad, though he couldn't figure out why. Something about him felt so oddly comforting, and almost familiar, that when the performance was over, Euphy felt compelled to ask about him.

First, he tried the man coming through the crowd, who held a hat out for donations, and who only said "You don't need names to pay for what you watched," when Euphy asked him who the dignified stranger was. Next, he asked a younger man with wide eyes and a soft, smiling mouth.

"I'm looking for someone. The leader of your group, maybe," he explained.

"You were just talking to him," the dancer pointed to the coin collector who was moving to the other side of the crowd.

Euphy looked around until he spotted the dignified man. "I meant him."

"Oh, he's not the leader. What do you want him for?"

What could Euphy say? He himself didn't really know why it felt so important to meet this person.

"No reason, I guess. He just…impressed me, is all."

The young man looked at Euphy thoughtfully. "We don't meet with people after the shows, and we've got a lot to take care of here, so it'd be better if you went on your way. Sorry," he finished with an apologetic shrug.

Euphy was starting to feel that if he didn't talk to the man now, he would forever lose his chance. Much of the crowd had already dispersed, and the performers were likewise starting to disappear into the darkness. The whole troupe would likely be gone tomorrow, travelling on to some new town and out of Euphy's reach. He made up his mind that he would simply have to approach the man himself.

By this time, the young dancer had moved some distance off, and was standing with his head bowed close to a woman holding a tambourine, apparently telling her something important, for she was listening to him intently.

Euphy pushed his way through the remnants of the spectators, reaching his mark just as the man was about to cross under the ropes which appeared to mark the border of the dancers' camp.

"Excuse me," he called to the figure. "Can I ask you something?"

"You could, but could I ask who you are?" asked the man as he turned to face Euphy.

"Um, I'm Euphemio," Euphy faltered. He hadn't thought about the fact that he would have to tell this man anything about himself.

The man seemed taken aback for a moment. People usually were, just like the librarian this afternoon. There were few people who didn't have some comment about his name when they first heard it.

"It's a fancy name, I know. I don't know anyone else with it." Euphy said,

"It's a fine name. You should be proud of it. I'd wager you'd miss it if it were gone."

"...Thanks," said Euphy absently, for when the man had interrupted him, he felt more than ever that they knew each other from somewhere. But where would he have met anyone from out of town? He'd spent his whole life here in Palomba Valley.

"Trouble, Golden?" asked a tall dancer who approached them, then, looking at Euphy. "This area's for troupe members only."

"Let him stay," said the man called Golden. "I'd like to talk to him."

"Where did you learn to dance like that?" Euphy asked, searching for some way to lead up to the questions he really wanted to ask.

"From many places, I suppose," answered the man, and Euphy couldn't tell if he were trying to be cryptic or not.

"Well, thanks for, uh, giving us some entertainment. We don't get too much of that around here. Or at least *I* don't." Euphy could feel the threads of his chance slipping away from him as he floundered for the words to say.

"Very good, Euphemio," said Golden with a slight bow. And there was something in it which felt more like a memory than an introduction. Something that reminded him of a sunny day, and a white horse shining on a green field, and he heard himself asking, "Actually, did you ever...spend time at the castle?"

"Which castle?"

Euphy blushed. To him, simple and untravelled as he was, there was only one castle. But someone like a roving performer – or a prince – must have seen a few.

"The one here. Prisma. That used to belong to you."

"I can't say I've owned a castle before," Golden answered with a laugh. It was laughter that sounded like water in a stream. The prince who had hired him to work in the stable had laughed the same way. There were more rocks in it now, more points where the water broke over rough spots, but it was the same sound.

"You *have*, though." Euphy insisted.

"You'd know more about that castle than me, if you still – " Golden stopped, but every move, every word now was giving him away.

"If I still work there, you mean?" Euphy finished for him. "So you remember me. I do still work there, by the way. In the stable."

Before the prince could answer, Euphy felt his arms being pinned behind him. From the corner of his eye, he saw that the person who held him was the coin collector from earlier.

"Can't let you go telling tales about us, if you work at the castle," the man growled.

"Castan," Golden spoke to call him off.

The man called Castan protested. "Haven't I told you again and again that this would happen? You're not careful enough."

Euphy could see other dancers giving wary glances at the commotion, and the gentle-eyed youth from earlier huffed onto scene, haranguing Castan as he did.

"I *knew* you were going to overreact! All I meant was that we should keep an eye out. Can't you listen to a complete sentence before rushing off to beat people's brains in?"

"Not when those people work in Livio's stable, and *smell* like it," Castan answered, tightening his hold on Euphy.

"Maybe you wouldn't notice it so much if you'd get off me," Euphy retorted.

"Castan, pay closer attention," Golden spoke. "You can smell horses on him, but is it the scent of fright-ened horses?"

Euphy was admittedly uncomfortable as Castan inhaled the air next to his ear.

"No," Castan said finally. "There's some other smell on him, too. Something wilder than horses. But whatever it is, it's not a frightened animal."

"Wouldn't you be frightened if you were held captive, and you thought the person in charge of you would hurt you?"

"Of course I would."

"Yet this one isn't."

Euphy felt a small surge of warmth to think that the unicorn was not afraid of him. Even if it didn't like him, it at least trusted him to take care of it.

"So what? It's his job not to hurt the horses. Doesn't mean he won't do it to anyone else."

"I'm asking you, as a favor. Please let him go."

With a grunt, Castan complied.

Euphy shook his arms, not making an effort to avoid hitting Castan with his elbow as he did so.

"Bridle, would you help Castan do the nightly rounds?" the prince – Golden – Vanya said to the young man who hovered at the edges of the scene.

Bridle looked as if he really would rather not, sending an imploring look to Vanya, and Castan didn't look much more pleased either.

"I'll take care of it if things get out of hand," said the tall dancer who was still standing next to Vanya. "Go on."

Euphy could hear the two arguing as they walked away.

"Castan prefers being safe to being sorry," Vanya explained once they were gone. "Did he hurt you?"

"Why did you say you haven't owned a castle?" Euphy blurted out, too full of his own questions to bother answering Vanya's.

"Because I haven't. When I lived in Prisma, it belonged to my father."

"But it should be yours now, since your father's…" he worried that it would be insensitive to say it.

"Dead?" Vanya supplied.

"Well, yes. And you're *supposed* to be. How are you still here?"

"That is quite a long story. Come back tomorrow, and we'll talk more."

But Euphy couldn't imagine leaving so soon. He was sure he'd come back tomorrow and find all of this gone, evaporated back into whatever dream world it had come from.

"Do your friends know? About you?" he asked.

"They do," replied Vanya. "But it isn't something we advertise."

"I can tell," said Euphy, thinking of Castan's aggressive form of welcome. "But you'll have to advertise it once you take your crown back."

"I fear I'm ill-suited for something like that. I'm not much good for anything after all this time."

"You mean you're not here to get rid of Livio?" Euphy felt his newborn hope draining away with Vanya's reply. It had felt natural to him that a long-lost prince returning to his country would want to reclaim it, would *have* to reclaim it. Who else was fit to do it if not him? Nobody in twenty years had been able to.

"Then why are you here? Why did you come back?"

Vanya's gaze flicked to the distance behind Euphy, who followed it to see Castan prowling back, without his young partner.

"*That has to be the shortest nightly round I've ever seen*," Euphy thought. His own rounds at the stable definitely took longer than the few minutes that had passed.

"I think you had better go unless we want another incident," said Vanya.

"But you're the prince. Why don't you just order him to leave us alone again?"

"Go on," he urged.

"Can you promise that you'll be here tomorrow?"

"I can't promise any of us will be here tomorrow." A note of sorrow broke through the urgency in his voice. "Though I have no plans to leave if I can help it."

"But –"

"I swear it on my family's graves."

It all felt very wrong to leave without knowing where Vanya had been, why he had come back, or how any of this was even possible. But what could he do? Shout and make a fuss so that Castan and all the others would come down on him? Plant his feet and refuse to do what a prince had ordered him to? Doubt the word of a man who bound it to the graves of his murdered relatives?

With the feeling of waking up from a dream, he turned and headed toward the looming shadow of the castle across the field, the small circle of lights fading into the distance behind him.

CHAPTER 6
Pizzica

The sun had risen and set, and Euphy walked the path back to where the camp had been last night, convinced that he would find only an empty clearing there.

But when he returned, the strange, shadowy figures moved again through the torchlight, and Vanya – or Golden, as he apparently preferred to be called now – took him within the borders of the troupe's village of tents. They entered one that looked like all the others on the outside, but the inside was adorned with blue banners of varying states of integrity. Many of them bore holes, were ragged on the edges, or were faded to the point that the embroidered patterns on them were difficult to make out.

Euphy looked closer and found that these dull threads had once been silver, and that they'd been worked into a pattern of waves on the blue. These had been the banners of King Nereus.

"I thought all of these were destroyed," Euphy said. "I watched them burning in the bonfires after you...left. Did you save these from the castle yourself?"

"These are ones that others kept, or made, and have brought to me. They insist on hanging them here, but sometimes it makes me feel worse. It makes me remember how I hadn't the strength to save anything but myself that night."

"There wasn't time to save anyone. I remember." Euphy tried to assure him. "We woke up one morning and

33

everything had changed overnight. Your family was suddenly gone, but we were told it was because you'd all been killed. How did you get out?"

Golden spun him the tale of how he'd seen his father fall, and cut his way through the invasion by desperation alone, but found that once he'd escaped, he was utterly unprepared to support himself in a world outside of castle walls. He had drifted through the wilderness in loneliness and poverty, until having joined the wandering morrismen a few years prior.

"But you're a prince. You seemed so capable to me back then," Euphy said, trying to reconcile the blithe, laughing man he had known with the melancholy one before him.

"Oh, I was trained in a great many things as a prince. I thought I was very competent back then. I was able to do all the things I'd been expected to do at the time, but out here, nobody has any use for courtly accomplishments. I couldn't even become a hunter for hire, for I'd been used to having dogs to sniff out the trail for me, and all I'd had to do was follow. I had no idea how to find a trail on my own.

I had a little skill with a sword, but I couldn't join the army. Any that was left by then belonged to Livio, and would have led me right back to the place I'd escaped from. I'd had more than my fill of fighting by then, in any case."

"Didn't anyone try to help you find your way? I can't be the first person to suggest you fight back against Livio."

Golden sighed. "I was so sheltered at home that nobody recognized me, and I didn't want to reveal my true self to anyone. I was afraid that someone would turn me back over to the Iron Hand."

"Are you afraid of him now? Being so close to home again?"

"I shouldn't be."

It was hard to tell with the dark makeup on his face, but Euphy could swear the man was crying. He was almost sure he saw golden drops glimmering on black paint in the torchlight.

The prince named Vanya was thought to have been resting peacefully since Livio had come to power. But he'd come back neither resting nor peaceful, not as the smiling prince, but a sorrowing vagabond. What a terrible conclusion to what would in any other circumstance have been considered a happy ending.

Euphy travelled home with these thoughts in his mind, and with the sounds of the unicorn stamping in its pen filling his ears, he slept. But rather than keeping him awake, they made him sleep too deeply, for he was greeted in the morning by Dario announcing, "Forgive me for disturbing your rest, *your highness*, but it is ten o'clock in the morning. If it weren't for the prince, I'd throw you out this minute."

Dario often told him things like this, but a bolt of wariness ran through Euphy, considering the secret of the camp outside the market. Did Dario know about that? Was that why he was bringing it up this time?

"If he hadn't hired you himself, I'd have sent you packing a long time ago. But I can't go against his word. It was one of the last orders he gave me."

Dario had remained loyal to Vanya, even believing him dead for two decades. But how would he would feel if he really did know what and where Vanya was now? Would he still care about the man the prince had become?

Did someone still represent the glory of the old days if they were no longer the same person they were back then? What did it mean to be the same person, anyway? Vanya was still the son of Nereus. He still had the same genteel carriage, though it was buried under rags, and that same bubbling laugh, though it was far rarer now. Was that enough?

But Euphy couldn't ask Dario's opinion on any of this. He hadn't been given permission to tell anyone about Vanya, and even if he had, the fact that they were within Livio's domain meant that he couldn't risk it.

"Castan doesn't want me to allow you back here anymore," Vanya told him when they were sat across from each other again, in the tent strung with blue and silver banners. "But given that no one's come to tear apart our little campsite yet, I assume this means you haven't shared what you know."

"Of course I haven't," Euphy said. "But where's Castan? Why isn't he here to make sure I don't do anything against you here?"

"He's waiting just outside," Vanya answered. "He agreed to stay out if I gave him permission to look in here when you came, so that he could easily come kill you if you tried to attack me."

"Oh," said Euphy, trying not to squirm at the thought that Castan's eye was probably glaring at his back through the curtain flap right now. "Do you know that's the second person you've protected me from? The only reason I haven't lost my job is because Dario won't go against the order you gave him to keep me on."

"Faithful Dario. But why should he want to get rid of you?"

"I – " Euphy scratched his head, hesitating to admit a fault in front of the prince. "Sometimes I don't get along with him so well."

"Not even now?" Vanya asked. "You must learn to tame your temper."

"You don't think I know that?" Euphy started to say, but he looked at the prince's eyes and felt it die.

The sensation was, in a way, the same as looking at the unicorn – both of them had eyes that looked back at him with the weight of things that he had never known. Eyes for whom these little flares of emotion, so consuming to Euphy, seemed a small and sad compared to the greater destruction they had witnessed.

It was unfair, though. The prince and the unicorn had both seen the world and all its tragedies. But to Euphy, the stable had been his world for nearly his whole life. Where was he supposed to get the knowledge they had?

The one person who didn't seem to carry the world in his gaze these days was the sunny young man who had, Euphy deduced, first tipped Castan off to Euphy's intentions. He didn't look his sunniest, though, when Euphy came upon him again, being scolded, unsurprisingly, by Castan.

"Why didn't you stop him?" Euphy heard Castan saying. "Why do I have to do everything for you?"

"I came and told you as soon as I heard him asking after Golden, didn't I? Excuse me for thinking you'd be someone I could trust to handle it," the young man countered, his jaw sticking out defensively.

"The point is that *you* ought to be able to handle things, too."

"Well, I agree that I made a mistake, seeing how you lost your mind and went on the warpath without even considering any other possibilities."

Castan gave him a shove and ordered him out of his sight, before stalking off himself.

Euphy knew what it was like to deal with that kind of scolding, and tried to offer a few words of support this fellow sufferer.

"Sorry I couldn't explain it to you before. Golden is a friend of mine from when I was younger," he explained. "I just wanted to see him again."

"That doesn't stop Castan from complaining about it," the young man said.

"I get the feeling he complains about a lot."

"You figured that out already, huh? You don't know how often I hear 'Bridle! You don't know anything,' or "You're doing it wrong!"

"Bridle," Euphy remembered Vanya calling him by the same word – one that was familiar enough to Euphy. "That's your name, isn't it?"

"Bridle Bishop. That's me, sure enough."

"Do you have much to do with horses?"

"Not horses. Sheep. I grew up as a shepherd."

"Then we're not too different. I'm a stablehand."

"Really? Then please come and talk with me about it some more. Not that I miss it all that much, but it'd be nice to have someone else who understands what it's like once in a while."

"Golden used to be interested in that sort of thing," Euphy said, remembering the interest Vanya had taken in a young boy's fascination with horses. "He won't listen?"

"He will, but it's not the same if you haven't done it yourself. And half the time, it's like he's thinking about something else, anyway. But he gets like that with everyone. Was he like that back when you knew him?"

"Not that I remember."

Euphy didn't like to dwell on the unhappiness that brought Vanya to where he was now. So he asked about the changes Bridle had gone through instead.

"How did you go from being a shepherd to being a dancer?"

"Working with sheep, you get pretty good at making a whole herd of creatures move together," Bridle said. "And I had to be pretty agile myself to keep the straying ones from going too far. So that sort of thing comes in handy around when you're trying to teach a bunch of people to step in time with each other."

But when Euphy had gone home, not all those in the camp were perfectly in step with each other.

"So now you're making friends with people who work for Livio?" Castan asked him.

"Golden was friends with him first," Bridle protested. "Besides, wouldn't it be good if we could have an ally in

38

the castle? We'd have someone who could tell us what's going on in there."

"Castan, you know that Bridle has a head for strategy," Golden put in. "It's why we brought him on in the first place. Can you trust his judgement now?"

"There's a difference between what he was brought on to do and what *this* is. Judging someone's motivations takes different work than knowing where to put them on a battlefield. "

"Then can you trust *my* judgement? Because *I* trust Euphy, and I've known him since he was a child," Golden said.

"You knew him *when* he was a child. Not since. Things change in that amount of time. People change."

"How well aware I am of that," sighed Golden. "But he is the last link to whomever I used to be. You set great store by the person I was then, don't you?"

"Yes, I do, and it's the same person you are now. I wish you wouldn't talk as if you and your old self were two different people."

"Then please show Euphy the same courtesy."

Bridle *thought* that he and Golden had carried their point, and Golden had sounded almost imperious there for a moment, right up until the moment his eyes had filled up with tears.

"Why is it so easy for you to believe that Euphemio is the same as before, but you can't believe it about yourself?" Castan asked, and to Bridle's utter discomfort, he himself was getting choked up as he spoke the question.

Bridle wondered what he ought to do if both of them were to start crying right there. With Golden, it was common enough, but Castan would probably be twice as rough on him later for having witnessed him in a vulnerable moment.

Never mind the fact that Bridle's own feelings had been hurt by Castan's remarks many times (though he would throw himself into the river that ran by the market before

39

he'd ever let himself show it in front of Castan). No, Golden was the only one who could be anything but his best in front of Castan without being scolded to death for it.

He was saved from deciding by the arrival of Vitalia, the tambourine player who, if she noted the attitudes of the other two as she passed by, didn't comment on it.

"Bridle, there you are!" she called cheerfully instead. "The new recruits want to practice the pizzica. We need you to teach them the steps."

"The pizzica, huh?" he mused as he gratefully followed Vitalia away. "That's about *all* we'll be good for if we don't get ourselves together soon."

"Don't tell me you're backing out now," she said.

"Of course not. But I don't see how we can take back a kingdom if the king we're trying to put on the throne doesn't believe he can do it, and none of us can even agree on how to get him there in the first place.

I mean, we've come this far – we're just about at the foot of Prisma, and we haven't even gotten past arguing about what exactly any of our roles are. Do you know that Castan still doesn't fully trust me to make decisions? He said so himself a minute ago."

Bridle gestured back to the direction they had just come. "And if he doesn't trust me – me, whose job is to draw up the battle lines in the first place – then how does he think we're going to have any chance of getting inside the castle? Just have everybody scramble and see if someone makes it in by luck?"

"Well, try to forget it for now. They really do want to learn the pizzica. I wasn't just making that up to get you out of there."

"Why don't you ask Castan to teach it, since he thinks he knows so much more than me?"

Vitalia didn't say anything more, for whatever she could say wouldn't alter the fact that Bridle was right. Something was going to have to change soon. If they had any chance of overturning Livio's rule and putting the rightful ruler back on the throne, it wasn't going to be accomplished by fighting amongst themselves.

When they'd started, they had been so united in their goals, but things were falling apart just when they were in sight of their objective.

Golden hadn't been very bold to start with, but being in sight of the castle was paralyzing him more each day, which made Castan fiercer and crueler, as if to make up for the lack in the one who was supposed to be the jewel of all they hoped for.

Castan's barbs were in turn putting a chip on bright Bridle's shoulder, so that he frequently slipped from his usual demeanor into darker episodes like this. And he wasn't alone. Lieutenant Sterling had yelled more at the young recruits in the past month than he had in the whole time Vitalia had known him, and her own first lieutenant, Diana, had just about worn holes in the Command Room's rug all the pacing she'd been doing these days.

After all the years they'd spent scouring the country, looking for those loyal to the House of Nereus, under the pretense of being a travelling troupe of simple performers in rags – would it all be for nothing? All the hours they'd spent practicing battle tactics and formations under the guise of morris dancing, or "moresca", as it had been called in the old Ausonia language. which conveniently allowed them to obscure their identities with its traditions of face painting and miming of warfare – would all of it go to waste, with everything falling apart here at the last hour? Vitalia could see one of three answers to these questions:

One: They would find some magic solution to their problems and would be able to successfully reclaim the kingdom.

Two: They would be unable to fix their crumbling unity, and retreat to wander the world again for who knew how long before making another attempt at overthrowing Livio.

41

Three: They would not fix their problems, but would try to take the castle anyway, and the Albionites would have a second night of glory to claim.

By now, she and Bridle had almost reached the practice ground where the new dancers awaited their lesson, and the musicians were re-tuning the strings of their instruments to provide the tune for them. Vitalia picked up her tambourine, but half-heartedly tapped in time with the words that she sang, about love not being enough to prevent separation, about moving when you ought to have stood still, and ending with nothing but a plea to be remembered.

She had never given much weight to the words before; but they felt eerily prophetic tonight, fitting the sad condition of their band, and echoing what their ghosts would surely wail after Livio slaughtered each of them.

"*I shouldn't have come, but now I'm here. Be well again, but don't forget me.*

CHAPTER 7
The Gallery of Battles

In the hall which had once been the reception room of King Nereus, was the Gallery of Battles. The walls of the hall, long and high, were now covered with huge paintings depicting the Livio's many exploits in battle, not the least of which was the overthrow of his predecessor.

In the painting representing that incident was a dark-headed figure whose downturned mouth and fierce eyes were a match for Livio's as the two of them forced their way through a dark chamber whose blue and silver tapestries were torn and trampled under their feet.

Theodora stopped to look at the image, and after a long moment's inspection, turned to her companion, who didn't share her interest in it despite the fact that he was one of its subjects.

"Why, Dandy!" she exclaimed. "This is you. Were you really in a battle?"

"A long time ago," Dandy admitted. He didn't like this painting; this was the first time he'd looked at it in years.

He hadn't realized how young and brave he'd appeared in it, back when he'd first earned the moniker of "Morningstar" for the devastation he'd wrought on his enemies.

He wished he hadn't brought Theodora here, but she had learned of the gallery's existence through an offhand comment from Marta, her maid, and had asked him to take her to see it. He hadn't had the heart to refuse her, cloistered as she was.

It was one of her better days, when she was somewhat more aware of the world around her, and this was possibly the one time that Dandy didn't welcome such a day. Just at this moment, he hoped she wouldn't recover enough to realize just what the painting showed, aside from himself.

"You look different now," she said. "Your face is softer here," she reached up and traced the line of his jaw. "But I like you better this way," she went on, unprompted. "If you were in a battle, that means you could have been killed, and you would have stayed looking like that forever," she gestured to the painting. "But the way you look now means that you made it through. You've lived long enough to look different."

Dandy hated that he could not – could never – ask her whether she knew what she was really saying. For if he hadn't made it through the battle for New Glory, she would not be in the circumstances she was in now. She would have gone on living the life she ought to have had, with her father and her brother alive, and her mind intact.

"I like you much better the way you are now," she repeated.

"Do I look kinder?" Dandy asked. That was one change from the man in the picture he would welcome.

"You're always kind," Theodora said. "But yes, now you look it. I wonder what *I* looked like back then."

He honestly did not see a difference between the incognizant girl he'd found wandering the halls after the battle, and the woman who faced him now. If there had been any change through the years that had passed, he was incapable of seeing it. Her face still held the same sweetness of expression on the same sensitive features which had looked up to him with total dependence in those early days after he'd come to Ausonia.

It was painful to think that she didn't share the same memories of how things had been then, when she had clung to him as the only thing she could trust in a world that had turned upside down overnight, and he had felt so sorry for her that he had demanded to Livio's face that he be allowed to shelter her.

But her not remembering how they'd formed their bond was less painful than the alternative. For if she recalled it, she would also know whom the picture showed crumpled at the feet of the two conquerors.

In that respect, the picture wasn't quite correct. Nereus had gone down with little fanfare – that was what was helpful about ambush attacks in the night. But his son had fought for longer. He had stayed on his feet even after Dandy's sword had pierced his chest, and had continued fighting the soldiers which Dandy and Livio had left to clean up the mess while they dashed ahead toward the throne room. They hadn't wanted to waste their time on someone who was already dying when the throne itself, which was the real prize, remained unclaimed.

It had been a commendable effort from the prince, Dandy remembered, given that Vanya was pouring blood from the hole under his collarbone as they passed him. At the time, it had made Dandy proud to have felled a royal house whose prince fought so bravely and fiercely. Now, it filled him with regret for having taken something so noble out of the world.

Was it any marvel that Theodora's mind had removed all memory of that night? At times, he could almost envy her.

"You don't sometimes wish you could go back in time?" asked Dandy, who wished it often.

"If I did, I'd be going to a time when I wouldn't have known you, and what would I do without my Dandy?"

He wasn't sure if he could truly be "her Dandy" without her knowing this part of their history together, but he was certain that he could not be so with it

45

CHAPTER 8
Fantastica

Euphy had navigated the labyrinth to Omega twice more since the day he'd gotten his library card, but he had yet to find anything useful under the label of Onomastics.

Even *Classical Names from Legend and Antiquity* hadn't helped much, for all of the names in it were already attached to their own important stories, and it somehow didn't feel right to give the unicorn a name that wasn't all his own, to make him share his identity with anyone or anything else.

He looked over the same row of spines he had already examined many times, as if something new would have sprung up there between this time and the last. But when nothing showed itself, he was finally forced to admit that he would have to try some other part of the library.

"Are there any sections here about legends? Maybe on things that are supposed to be imaginary?" he asked Dandy, who was currently taking his turn with *Classical Names*, and not having much luck with his own search, if his furrowed brow were any indication.

"You could try 'Mythology'. Do you want me to help you find it?"

Dandy led him there, and Euphy was carrying an armload of books back to his room before long, but when he had the chance to read them, many simply told him what he'd already found out firsthand, and some of them were outright wrong in their assumptions.

The unicorn might have stepped out of the realm of legend, but it was still actual living thing. Surely there had been someone else, at some point in the world, who had seen a real live unicorn, and whose information would be more useful than these types of speculations and rumors.

He tried the library's Alpha corridor next, where he searched for "animals", and found plenty of resources for raising chickens and other barnyard animals, but still nothing like what he needed (though he made a note of some that could help with the other horses he cared for).

Dandy recommended the Zeta section for "zoology" on his next foray. This section was clearly less visited than the others, but maybe that meant there were more chances of finding something useful.

Amongst the slightly dusty titles, he noticed a worn green leather volume with faded gilt letters embossed on its cover:

RESEARCH IN FANTASTICA

He flipped it open and landed on a page describing "Behemoth" with detailed diagrams of the creature's muscular structures, including its huge, curved horns, advice on what to do when encountering them the wild, and a reports of a few brave souls through history who had tried to tame them.

Euphy's heart thumped to find real, practical advice about an animal which most people, including himself, would have doubted existed not too long ago.

His fingers flew toward the heading for the letter U, catching glimpses of entries for things like "Cockatrice" and "Leviathan" along the way.

He felt like he'd been running a race by the time he reached "Unicorn", with its illustration of a creature very like the one in the dungeon, tall and powerful, rather than the delicate, mincing things he'd formerly imagined. Whoever had painted it must have done so from experience.

48

A paragraph halfway down the page echoed his thoughts on the matter:

"In popular culture, there is a misunder- standing of the fundamental nature of unicorns. Most accounts focus on their sweetness and beauty, but this is an effect of the wildness in their hearts, as contradictory as this seems. There is a fire within them, and when someone stokes that ever-boiling fire, they turn it to one direction or the other.

When treated with kindness, a unicorn will grow so gentle that even young maidens may direct it.* But when treated with cruelty, the unicorn will become so savage that even warriors and kings cannot withstand its onslaught. Those who come in contact with a unicorn must be careful in which direction they turn its fire.

Coppelia of Jonani is the most well-known instance of such a phenomenon, and most representations of a unicorn resting with its head in a maiden's lap are derived from the account given in Carletto's **Rare Beasts of the Wild."*

Then, turning the page, Euphy caught his breath when he saw:

"Of particular importance if one wishes to influence a unicorn is to call it by its true name. To know a unicorn's name is to know its power, and is therefore not something that is easily discovered. If the beast decides someone has earned the right to know, it will reveal its name to that person. Considering that such trust is not given lightly, those who are worthy of it are generally not the type to reveal the name to any other person, and consequently, no known record of a unicorn's name exists."

So Euphy had been right. There was clearly something important related to unicorns and their names, and he was a little proud of himself for having figured at least that much out. It felt like a good sign that he might eventually be able to find the name he needed.

However, this small glow of positivity faltered when he was saw not with an ideal unicorn in a painting, but a distressed real one, standing upright and tossing his giant head, snorting in anger and pain.

He rushed to the gate. What had gone so wrong that the unicorn had been driven so fully out of its torpor? Just above the silver hooves, he saw red rings circling its pasterns, and thick liquid of the same color oozing out to mat the feathery fur which almost hid the heavy cuffs there. Cuffs against which the animal had clearly strained hard enough to rub his own skin raw with them.

Euphy dropped his book, using both hands to fumble for his keys and throw the gate open. The creature scarcely seemed to register his entry into the pen, as his gaze was focused up to the top of the high stone walls surrounding him.

Euphy followed it and saw, perched there like jaguar watching its prey, Stregatto, the same hunter who had been needling Dario about the carriage horses the morning after the unicorn had arrived.

"What happened?" Euphy demanded with a voice that caused the unicorn to toss his head with extra vigor, but Euphy did not break his gaze on Stregatto in spite of this.

"Can't rightly say," drawled the hunter, all affected innocence. "This animal must have lost its senses. Just started bucking and charging – or trying to – out of nowhere. He's kept at it for a good quarter of an hour now, though I don't know why he suddenly thought he could get out from those," he nodded to the blood-flecked irons.

"*Dumb* animal."

Euphy was willing to bet that half of this story was true. He had no doubt that the unicorn had been agitated for as long as Stregatto had said, but he was also certain that Stregatto had provoked him into it for his own entertainment.

"The king won't be pleased when he hears about this," Stregatto went on, grinning. "You neglecting your duties, and leaving his prized asset to ruin itself like this."

"If Livio's so concerned about it, why doesn't he come down here and take care of things himself?" Euphy snapped, knowing that he was going against all of Dario's warnings on safety in dealing with Livio's people, but the sight of the sores on Minari's beautiful feet had set him on edge.

Stregatto laughed. Seeing animals – and people – in distress apparently put him in a talkative mood.

"He's scared to death of the beast. He knows it would kill him if he got too close."

"Would serve him right," Euphy muttered. Then, because he was anxious to examine the unicorn's wounds, but not anxious to have Stregatto watch him do it, he called "You going to sit there and gape forever? Honestly, if you have nothing better to do than watch what a stablehand does all day, your life must be pretty pathetic."

He was counting on this to make Stregatto leave, because Euphy had never once heard a hunter pass up an opportunity to insult any of the palace staff, especially not those who had worked under Nereus, and suggesting that Stregatto would want to stay and watch someone who was both of those things, would be going against everything he had seen from the hunter so far.

The bid worked, and Stregatto disappeared from the top of the wall with something that sounded like "Giving yourself airs," but he scaled down and marched past the gate without so much as a second glance inside the pen.

Euphy knelt down to get a better view of the unicorn's feet, though he kept as much of a distance as he could, for his own safety's sake.

"Easy," he murmured in the tone with which he'd calmed many horses. But it was the first time he'd expected the words to be fully understood by the animal he was speaking to. "Please don't kick. I can't help you if you kick me."

He raised his eyes and saw that the unicorn had at least stopped tossing his head.

"I'm going to have to touch you in order to make you feel better," he explained. "I'll go as softly as I can, but please just tell me if I'm hurting you, alright?"

It gave the slightest dip of its head, as if it didn't want to acknowledge that it needed help, but Euphy took this as the closest thing to an answer he was going to get.

He lifted up the first of the unicorn's feathers, lightly, so as not to disturb the torn skin underneath.

It may have been the worst such wound he'd seen on an animal, given the fact that the unicorn had pulled against his irons with more strength than any horse ever could, and Euphy was going to have to work around and under those irons to treat him. But he couldn't let that frighten him. If he didn't heal these cuts, nobody else would or could, and if this animal – his animal – trusted him, then he had to be worthy of that trust.

He talked out loud through each step of the process to help steady both of their nerves. There was a nervous moment when the antiseptic went onto the cuts, and the unicorn's whole body jerked, while he made a sound that could have easily turned into one of the wild shrieks he'd made on the first night, but he bit it off – the first time Euphy had heard him willingly restraining such a reaction – and allowed himself nothing more than pained huffing until everything was over.

"There we are," Euphy said, rubbing his hands as gingerly over the bandages as he could, to make sure everything was snugly in place. "You'll have to try and move as little as possible, or else these'll get worn through by the metal. Can you do that?"

The unicorn gave the same stiff little bob of his head, and Euphy clambered up to emerge from the pen. When he had locked the gate, he found the gilded letters of *Research in Fantastica* glinting up from the ground where he had dropped it, and he wondered whether it contained anything regarding the nursing of a unicorn's wounds. Either way, he might have a thing or two to add to it.

It didn't occur to him until later that this had been the first time he'd entered into the unicorn's presence without hesitation. Of course, he had been cautious in dressing the wounds, but when he'd first arrived, first seen the signs of blood, he had charged in to help without thinking. And what was more, this was the first time the unicorn had allowed it.

Euphy did not go to see the morris troupe that night, feeling compelled to stay close by the unicorn, lest Stregatto or any of his friends felt like abusing him again.

He wanted to send a message to the dancers, but decided not to risk it. Best not to expose their connection to any watchful eyes in the palace. He hoped Vanya wouldn't be too disappointed.

He went to bed with the tears of a prince and the blood of a unicorn on his mind, but he awoke with something else having replaced them. A word, or more like a sound – "Min" – had formed there, and he couldn't tell where it had come from. All he knew was that it seemed to grow louder when he checked on the unicorn.

It wasn't the unicorn speaking to him. He would have known if he'd heard that voice of embers and metal. But was it possible that they could communicate by other means?

And if…if they were going tell something as important as their name, wouldn't they say it in a manner that nobody else could hear? Was this how it was done – not through words, but through an inexplicable feeling in his heart?

The book had said that unicorns would reveal their own names to those they deemed worthy. Had the problem with Stregatto yesterday convinced the unicorn that Euphy was one of those worthy ones? Euphy had simply done what he thought was right – he hadn't done it to get into the unicorn's good graces, but if that was the result, then something wonderful might have come out of the trouble in the end.

Could it really be as simple as that, though? Was "Min" really all there was to it? He didn't think someone as stubborn as the unicorn would give everything away so easily, but it was all he had, so it would have to do for now.

"Good morning…Min," he said quietly.

The unicorn stared at him.

"Is that your name? Was it you who told me?"

The unicorn said nothing, but in his eyes was a look that could almost be tolerance, and the difference was enchanting. It buoyed him up all through the rest of the day, even though the threat of Stregatto was still there and Min's bandages had to be changed again. Even though he still hadn't seen Vanya or the morrismen.

He had a name, or at least part of one, and he hadn't expected how much of a difference it would make not just to the unicorn, but also to himself.

CHAPTER 9
Cold and Raw the North Wind Blows

It was another full day before Euphy felt safe leaving Min for long enough to visit the morris camp. None of the hunters had come near in that time, so maybe the king really *had* heard what Stregatto had done, and had forbidden them from coming around again. That would be one thing to be thankful to Livio for, whatever else he may have done.

When Euphy ventured out that night, Vanya did not meet him at the camp. But when he introduced himself to a pair of morrismen who were standing at the entrance, they told him that he'd been expected.

"Euphy. Golden's been waiting for you."

"Are you sure this was the one he meant, Lazaro?" asked the other dancer.

"How many people do you know with a name like that? And he looks just like what Golden described." Then, turning to Euphy,

"Let me take you to him."

"I think I remember the way," Euphy said.

"All the same, wouldn't want you getting lost."

Euphy couldn't blame them. He would have done the same thing in their position. It was the same as how he couldn't stand the thought of someone getting close to Min without his being there to protect him.

"Golden's been better since you've been coming," Lazaro said companionably as they walked. "I think it helps him to have a friend."

Their path took them by one tent notably larger than the rest, from which voices could be heard. One of them was definitely Castan's, along with the unmistakably princely voice of Vanya.

It sounded as if Castan were lecturing him again, but there were other voices, too. Euphy could identify Bridle trying to make himself heard, and a woman among the group.

Lazaro looked troubled. "I guess they're not done with their meeting yet," he said, and attempted to take Euphy back the way they had come, but it didn't prevent them both from hearing Castan's remonstrative tones.

"There are plenty of regulars in the market who have no love for Livio. Being so close to where it all happened, they've seen more than enough of what he's like."

And then, the noble voice speaking in reply.

"That's exactly why we should *not* recruit them. They went through enough the first time. I can't ask them to commit to going through it again. If they've rebuilt their lives even through everything he's done, how can I ask them to trade that for another war and more uncertainty? Do I deserve such a sacrifice?"

"Who here thinks this is uncertain?" Castan asked, followed by multiple overlapping answers, among which was the woman's voice stating that Golden might not be so far off the mark just at this moment.

"You have no problem trusting people who accept the benefits of working in Livio's court, but you won't trust the people who've been suffering directly outside of it?"

It was clear to Euphy that Castan meant him, and he felt Lazaro's furtive glance on him.

"He is Ausonian, too," they heard Vanya say. "And he knew me as I was, when I truly was a prince, not as I am now. If anyone were to know me, to truly know what I'm worth, it would be him."

"So you still won't believe that the rest of us can know you the way you are now, and love you just as much? Only the things from your youth are worth anything to you, is that it? None of us have any value because we've come to you afterward?"

Vanya protested, but Castan didn't wait to listen. He threw back the tent canvas and Euphy was thrown off balance by the force with which Castan, unseeing, rushed past him.

He looked to Lazaro for a clue about what to do, but Lazaro's gaze had turned back to the ten In the entrance to the tent entrance, where Vanya stood, eyes tired and shoulders sagging.

He dismissed Lazaro and attempted a smile for Euphy (who privately thought it was a rather unsuccessful attempt), running a hand through his hair as if to push away the heaviness of the preceding scene.

"Euphy, how nice to see you again."

His tone was falsely casual, and Euphy tried to think of what to say. Ought he acknowledge what he'd just heard? Because it had sounded like they'd all been discussing something beyond Vanya returning to Prisma for simple nostalgia's sake.

Noting Euphy's dazed silence, Vanya's mask of innocence dissolved like thinnest paper.

"I suppose it won't do any good to ask how *much* of that you heard," he said, resignation filling his voice.

Euphy shook his head. "Why did you say you weren't here to take your throne back?"

"I'm really not fit to do it. I was telling the truth about that. Though Castan believes I can. You heard just how desperately he believes it. "

"I guess Bridle is part of this, too? And the others…"

An idea was dawning on him. Just how many "others" were there? Was the whole of this camp involved in the scheme? Was that why Lazaro had to escort him here? Was that why Castan was so zealous about keeping outsiders away? Were every one of these seemingly simple morrismen really here to depose Livio?

Vanya affirmed each of these questions, and Euphy managed to reply in spite of his head spinning at the notion.

"I don't think so many people would support you without a good reason to think you could do it." He chose not to mention the voice of the doubting woman he had heard.

"Don't you see?" Vanya asked, his voice growing thin. "That's what makes it more difficult. The more people count on me, the higher the stakes rise. If I can't do it, I'll be responsible for destroying so many other people's dreams, the way mine were destroyed. I'll have failed my country and my people, twice. I'm not sure I'll survive it a second time."

Euphy had meant to encourage him, but what should he do when even encouraging words brought Vanya lower, and brought more golden tears to his green eyes?

"Why don't we go to your tent?" Euphy fumbled for something to say. "Maybe if you had some tea or –"

He felt ridiculous, but Vanya nodded, and Euphy awkwardly led the way to Vanya's tent, where was he relieved to see a tea set was actually set out.

The tea was going to have to be cold, since starting a fire felt beyond all of Euphy's capabilities just at the moment.

Vanya didn't complain, but obediently drank what he was given. "There's no one else I can really talk to about what's on my mind," he said. "Castan tries to listen, but he's so focused on the future, and what I ought to do to improve it, that he doesn't appreciate how it feels to need to mourn the past.

It's not that I don't care about the people who know me now, but they don't know how I was in those days, so they don't know how far I've really fallen. They don't know how much work it's going to take to get back to the way I once was, assuming I ever do. Nobody but you has seen all of that."

Vanya looked into his teacup. "If I were a stronger leader, we might have already liberated the country by now, and this could all have been over. If I were stronger, we might not have needed to liberate it in the first place. "

Here, Euphy found a thread to pick up. Even if Vanya hadn't been strong enough to stop Livio back then, he *had* been strong enough to get himself out alive. That had to count for something.

"How did you do it last time? How did you survive on the night when Livio came?"

Vanya's voice grew as grim and cold as his tea when he said "I cut my way out and left my father's body behind. I survived because I focused on saving myself and no one else."

"But there couldn't have been time to save him. He fell first, didn't he? And it wasn't as if you could have dragged him out. If you had stopped for him, you would have died, too."

"But I would have died with a good name. I would have had a clear conscience, and my father would not have died thinking I didn't care."

"I don't think he thought that," Euphy ventured carefully. He didn't really know what their relationship had been like, but given how happy Vanya had been back then, he seemed like a safe bet to say so.

"I often wonder whether I showed him I loved him enough. Back then, it hadn't yet occurred to me that I would someday have to take care of myself, let alone anyone else. My father seemed so strong that I never thought much about what would happen when he died, and whenever I did think about it, I assumed I would have all of the court advisers around me to help me know what to do.

I always had so many other people to look after my needs, and I didn't really know how much work it was for them. If

I had realized any of that at the time, I might have thanked my father for it."

Euphy tried to imagine the blithe, laughing prince fighting his way through bloody battle, learning to live in the cold, harsh world all by himself, trying to face burdens he hadn't even known existed.

He thought about what it would feel like to have his entire world ripped away in a moment, and the sensation actually felt a lot like what he'd experienced when he'd had to leave Min that evening.

"I never even found out what happened to my sister," Vanya spoke again. "Whether she died first, or whether I could have saved her in time, if I had tried."

Euphy looked down. Even if he had known anything about the fate of Vanya's sister – Theodora was said to have been her name – it didn't seem like it would help. Vanya was wandering in a black fog alone.

"I'm older now than my father was when I was born. Do you suppose I'll ever live up to him?"

If only calling Vanya by his true name could help him the way it would help the unicorn. But knowing that Golden had once been Vanya did the opposite for him. He only considered himself all the more worthless knowing the place he had been cast down from.

Finally, Euphy muttered something that sounded pitiful even to him about needing to get home, and stumbled out of the tent, past the Lazaro and his partner still on watch, and onto the dark path toward Prisma.

When he had come this way from the castle, his greatest concern had been how long it would take him to get back to Min. He'd had no knowledge of the morrismen's true objectives, nor of the true weight of responsibility which Vanya carried alongside his guilt and remorse.

He hadn't known he would somehow become responsible for restoring two poor creatures, both torn from the worlds they had been born to and locked into a contest for power through no desire of their own, and both looking to him to help them endure their battles.

And if there was to be a battle for power – the realization sliced into him – it was one that not everyone might survive. It would have been bad enough for Livio simply to elevate himself by using Min. It was going to be so much worse if anyone tried to oppose him in it, especially a broken prince who didn't even have the strength the fight against his own memories, much less against the man who had destroyed them in a matter of mere hours.

Vanya had been right when he'd said Euphy was the sole person who knew all sides of the story. Not even Vanya himself knew about Min, or of Livio's plans. But if Euphy were to warn the morrismen, it would open Min up to a whole new set of dangers. The more people who knew about Min and his supposed ability to lend power, the higher the chance that more than just Livio would come seeking it for themselves.

On the other hand, if Euphy didn't warn them, he would be letting them walk into a situation far worse than what they were already struggling to prepare for.

How could he save everyone? It felt like all of this could hardly be accomplished by a mere stablehand, not even by one with so lofty a name as Euphemio.

CHAPTER 10
Bleak in the Morning Early

The room was dark, the hour was early, and Euphy had barely slept at all. After a point, he gave up trying and grabbed *Research in Fantastica*. He knew it wouldn't have any information on whether it was right to reveal the existence of a mythical beast if it meant saving the lives of a rebel army, but flipping the pages at least made him feel like he was doing something to figure it out.

In the *General Information* chapter, he came across a passage which had nothing to do with his current question, but perhaps held the answer to another one:

"Just as iron is widely known to suppress the power of these creatures, and has been used to hamper their health and abilities, the same principle renders man-made remedies less than effective in aiding and restoring the same.

What is not widely known is that iron in its raw form does no harm to these creatures, for both are naturally occurring entities, born of the earth, and are therefore of like makeup. It is only once the metal has been worked by human hands that it takes on the limiting properties for which it has become famous.

With this in mind, those who find themselves in the rare position of nursing any of the species described in this work are advised to use natural remedies to the extent possible, in place of those devised by chemists. Honey, in particular, has been observed to possess advanced healing properties."

Well. That was something useful. He didn't have the answers to everything yet, but this could at least help with one thing. Min hadn't been recovering as much as Euphy would've liked. He'd been eating only slightly more than before, which wasn't saying much, especially now when he needed good nutrition to heal from those awful lacerations. If Euphy could bring him something like honey, maybe it would cheer him up enough to eat the way he ought to.

It was easier to fall asleep now that he had some plan of action, and in the morning, he hurried back down the path which had been so dark and cold last night, but which felt quite different lit by the early rays of the sun.

He ventured into the luxuries corner of Clockface, gripping the pocketbook which was stuffed with every spare coin Euphy had, and was glad to find a booth selling honey, though the amber jars he saw there were labelled *Sugared Honey*.

This wouldn't work. The fact that they'd had extra sugar added to them before they came to market probably disqualified them from being called "natural."

With a thump, Euphy set down the jar he'd been holding. Who in the world had such extravagant tastes that they tried to improve on something which was already so much of a delicacy that most people couldn't afford it?

He slid the jars to the side and found behind them, a group labelled *Raw Honey*. However, these jars were also twice the price of the others.

Euphy felt as if the luxury market followed less logic than the library. Why ask *more* to for an item that had *less* work put into it?

"That variety is excellent for maintaining good health," the vendor told him.

"I know," Euphy muttered under his breath, "but it's not so excellent for maintaining my pocketbook." The truth was that he simply wasn't going to be able to afford this.

He turned away, telling himself that honey could not be the only healthy or natural thing sold here. He'd been to this market hundreds of times; what else had he seen that he could use? Not the cinnamon and sugar sold by the pound to his right, nor the cakes and bubbling drinks being sold to his left. He would have to get out of the sweets aisle if he wanted to find anything helpful.

As he debated where to go, a familiar voice called his name, and Bridle jogged up to him, waving excitedly.

It was the first time Euphy had seen in the sunlight rather than the evening's dying glow, and without at least a few traces of black paint smeared across his face. Looking at him the light of day, no one would have guessed he was planning to overthrow a government, and he showed no signs of the seriousness Euphy had heard from the other side of the tent canvas last night.

"Euphy! How've you been? Feels like I haven't seen you in forever."

Did Bridle know that the morrismen's secret was out? That Euphy knew what they were really doing behind the façade?

"I tried to come by last night, but…" Euphy was unsure how to finish.

"Oh, Golden told me that you, um, learned some of our dance steps. You-know-who was fit to be tied, as usual," he rolled his eyes. "But I say the more, the merrier. It's not like we were getting very far with the way things were before. I think it wouldn't hurt to have some new ideas to help us along."

Euphy felt a twinge of guilt pull at him. He did know of something very important which could help them, but he couldn't tell them about it.

"What are you doing in the market so early?" Bridle went on. "We don't normally see you around here until nightfall."

"One of my animals is sick and hurt. I thought something fresh to eat might help him."

"Your favorite?"

"You could say that." Euphy chose his words carefully. How could he even compare the other horses with Min? It almost didn't feel fair to them.

"I heard that hesitation. I know we shouldn't have favorites, but sometimes it happens, right?" Bridle shot him a conspiratorial smile.

"I had some in every flock. Though I have to say I had some definite 'least favorites', too. Little Peter, for one. " His brow furrowed with the memory of the mischief Little Peter had evidently caused.

"How did you learn his name?" Euphy asked.

"I made it up, of course. What, did you think he told it to me himself?"

Euphy had been so caught up in discovering Min's name – which the animal could definitely choose to tell or not – that for a moment he forgot it wasn't the normal way of doing things.

"Anyway, you're here to get something to help your favorite horse back on its feet," Bridle said, and Euphy was grateful for the way he was willing to carry a conversation alone, and how his mind seemed to be brimming with so many thoughts that he didn't tend to stay on any one topic for long. "What were you thinking of giving it?"

Euphy remembered just then that he could easily do for Min what he sometimes did for the other horses.

"Feeding them fruits and vegetables is healthy once in a while."

"Hmm, if you say so. Out in the fields, we didn't have the royal budget to give the flock many treats, though I *can* tell you not to feed them broccoli. It'll give them goiters. Do horses get goiters? By the way, what's down those little streets?" Bridle finished as he walked alongside Euphy, looking at the lanes of brick-and-mortar shops which radiated out from the plaza housing the stalls, each lane finding its end in the alley which ran along the market's encircling wall.

"Those are for people richer than me. That's where you get handbags that cost a week's pay, and jewelry that costs a month's."

"And the wall? Wouldn't that be a hazard in an emergency, with just one way out and all?"

"That's the point. It's so that you can't get out without having to pass by all the store windows on the way. The idea is that you'll get convinced to buy something if you have to see it over and over."

"Aha. Can't say it's a bad strategy, even if it is bad for the rest of our wallets. Maneuvering people into positions that work best for you and worst for them. It's what I would do. Speaking of maneuvering, look at that. That would've been me a few years back."

He motioned toward a boy leading a line of sheep at the far end of Ninth Street, looking as if he'd gotten turned around his way to the livestock pens in the plaza, which were nearer to Second Street.

Bridle leaned forward to watch as the ram of the group, having taken into its head that it did not want to go market, abruptly stopped and dug its feet into the ground, resisting the boy's efforts to pull to along with his shepherd's crook.

By the time the ram moved again, Bridle was counting to himself, apparently out of habit.

"There's one missing," he said, then trotted forward and called out loud.

"Hey, count your stock. Didn't you have nineteen?"

The boy looked over his little flock, and though Euphy lost count when he tried to tally them himself, he assumed that there were at most eighteen there.

"It has to be in the alley. I'll help you look," Bridle told the boy. "You stay there, and I'll drive it back to you. Euphy, help him on this end."

He jogged up the road toward the alley, and Euphy dutifully waited for him to return with a straggling lamb. He hadn't expected Bridle to blow past, driving not a sheep before him, but a second boy, who was running with a stolen, bleating lamb in his arms.

The young thief's speed was slowed by the lamb's weight and squirming, and he hadn't counted on the rest of flock being spooked by the oncoming rush, which made them fan out and block the entrance to the plaza.

He tried skirting around them, but changed his mind the more they shifted, and turned to run back up the adjacent Tenth Street.

Bridle stopped to assess the situation next to Euphy. Chasing the boy up Twelfth Street would be pointless, given that he could reach the alley and simply take the next street back to the plaza before anyone could catch up with him. But if they waited in the plaza for him, he could simply choose to follow the alley all the way to the main exit.

"The exit! There's only the one. Let's get there before him!" Bridle put his head down and took off at a run straight through the rows of stalls.

Euphy followed, and they had not covered half of the space, darting around startled shoppers, when a chestnut horse thundered up alongside them.

The figure atop it, with fierce gaze and ramrod posture, was Dandy. "Euphy!" he shouted. "I can catch him faster. You go up Twelfth then down the alley on the right."

"You," he called, and Bridle stood up straight. "Take the left. Force him toward the plaza."

"But –"

"I can get across the space faster than he can. No matter which way he comes from, I can catch him. Now go." The note of authority in his voice sent them both running.

Within minutes, the thief had burst back into the open space. But his prolonged flight had tired him, and he moved even more slowly than before.

In contrast, Dandy's horse was in good form, and Dandy handled it deftly enough through the crowds that the boy was soon apprehended.

With one hand gripping the boy's collar, and the other holding the horse's reins, Dandy marched them both toward the guard's booth that was nestled into the wall near the exit.

Bridle and Euphy trailed after him, and the little shepherd with his flock trailed after them all, looking between Bridle, Euphy, and the stern man with the horse in awe.

After Dandy had handed the thief over to an officer posted outside the station with many serious words, he turned to group following behind him.

Euphy spoke first. "Bridle, this is Dandy. He's a friend from the castle."

Bridle bounced forward, breathless but smiling. "You know your strategy, sure enough. We need more of that type of decisiveness these days."

Euphy knew he was thinking of Vanya, who once would have been the equal of Dandy for fine horsemanship and panache.

Bridle extended his hand, introducing himself and asking, "Do you work in the stable, too?"

"No, I...look after one of courtiers."

"Oh, so a valet, then.

Before Dandy could respond, a second officer came from within the station to take their statements; the shepherd boy first, then Euphy and Bridle, and Dandy last.

While Dandy was busy answering his round of questions, Bridle leaned toward Euphy and asked quietly, "Listen, do you think he might be interested in what we're doing? In 'learning to dance', I mean? Someone like that, who knows what to do, who isn't scared to take action – we sure could use him, if we could get him on our side. Especially with the way things have been going lately."

Euphy wished he knew enough about Dandy to be able to answer that question. He knew that Dandy was helpful and knowledgeable, and going by what he'd done today, was a skilled strategist and horseman. But if he were a valet, what thoughts might he have regarding Livio? The courtiers would all be Livio's people; would Dandy be faithful to his master? Or was he, like Euphy, only a product of circumstance?

He said as much to Bridle, who apparently decided to find out right now, as the second Dandy finished with the officer, Bridle asked him "Did you live in the palace when King Nereus was there?"

"I didn't," said Dandy, gravely and simply. "I wish I had. Livio never should have come into Ausonia. He didn't have the right. I ought to have fought against it."

Euphy was surprised at this. It wasn't at all uncommon for Ausonian castle staff to feel that way, but they usually didn't say it openly, for fear of losing their jobs, or more.

Bridle shot Euphy a meaningful look.

The chestnut horse made a snuffing noise, and it dawned on Euphy then that he knew this animal.

"Why are you're riding Rusciu? I thought she belonged to a lady," he asked. The mare was relatively new to the stable, but the lady who owned it, whoever she was, had never come to ride it.

The serious look slipped from Dandy's face, and for half a moment, he looked almost bashful. "That lady asked me to buy it for her," he said, flipping the reins between his hands. "She's the one I look after, though her health doesn't let her ride much. I was actually taking Rusciu out for the first time since I bought her. First day out and she's already proven herself."

"I'd say!" Bridle agreed. "You and her both!"

"That's because she's had excellent care," Dandy said, gesturing toward Euphy.

Bridle beamed as much as if the compliment had been directed toward himself.

The clock tower rang fifteen minutes until nine, and Euphy jumped. The unexpected chase and meeting with Dandy had eaten away the hour, and he still hadn't gotten what he'd come for. He might just have time to get something for Min if he hurried, but he was going to have to sprint all the way back to the castle.

When he hastily explained his situation, Dandy asked "Why don't you take Rusciu? She knows you already, and you'll get there faster. I can walk back."

This was more than Euphy had even thought to ask for. Dandy had saved him from a tight spot once again.

He took the reins and was off, thinking again of that glowing image of a prince on a white horse, but thinking, too, of an apparent valet who carried himself like something more than a servant, who always appeared just when he was needed most, and always knew just what to do to fix a problem.

Maybe Bridle was on to something. Maybe Dandy could do something for the ragged band in the morris camp the way he always did for Euphy. Maybe he could do enough so that they wouldn't need Min's help at all.

CHAPTER 11
Mouths to Feed

As the horse pounded over the same green field where Vanya used to spark about like a comet, Euphy thought over his hurried choices back at the fruit stall, where he'd practically thrown his money at the vendor for apples, pears, carrots – whatever he could easily grab. He hadn't had the time to hesitate over any of it, though the fear had since crept into him that it would be insulting to offer Min some of these things. The carrots in particular.

Apples and pears could at least be taken in one bite, and eaten in a dignified manner, but the idea of Min crunching, bite by bite, through the long orange sticks, like some clumsy, common horse felt absurd.

After arriving home and taking care of his morning duties, he finally picked up his sack of goods and the doubts that came with it, and placed the offering – all except for the carrots – before Min with sweating hands.

He questioned himself a hundred times in that moment, but Min actually bent his noble head and began to eat, and Euphy fought back the urge to reach out and stroke the wavy mane in relief. He contented himself with watching how it began to glimmer just a fraction more than usual.

It wasn't long before Min had eaten everything, and Euphy only had the carrots left to offer. "I have these, but I didn't know if you would like them," he said.

Min nickered softly in what sounded like a laugh, and took the carrots from his hand as docilely as a rabbit. This time, Euphy actually had to clench his fist to keep himself from stroking the velvety ears that twitched inches from his face.

There was nothing ridiculous about this at all. He felt embarrassed now of having conjured up such thoughts as he had on the ride home. As if anything Min did could ever be absurd.

When the last bit of food was gone, and Euphy could think of no more excuses to stay, he at last turned to the gate.

But he looked over his shoulder again, and when he did, a new light shone into what he had thought was a familiar corner of his mind.

"I'll see you later…Minari," he said.

*   *   *

That night, for the first time, Euphy entered the "Command Room" – the tent which had been the scene of the argument he'd heard last night. This was where the dancers who were more than dancers planned their next moves in the plot to overthrow Livio.

They were to supposed to talk over the idea of recruiting Dandy to the group tonight, and Euphy just hoped that not every discussion ended with someone of the party fleeing in the kind of high emotion he'd seen last night.

He thought the same trick which had worked with Min might work to keep things calm in the Command Room, and he made his way back to the fruit vendor to buy the last batch of strawberries before the stall closed.

When he held his gift out to the group assembled in the tent, Castan and Bridle were standing around a central table along with a man who was unknown to him, and a woman whose voice it must have been that Euphy had heard doubting last night. Vanya hadn't joined them yet, and Euphy couldn't help thinking that maybe he was elsewhere trying to compose himself into something other than a tearful mess.

Castan stared at him, and asked flatly, "What is that?"

"It's a – " Bridle started helpfully, but Castan cut him off.

"I know what it is," he said, and turned back to Euphy. "What did you bring it for?"

"As a host gift."

Castan's face softened by a single degree, and he said "That's good of you, but…"

At the same time, Bridle grinned and reached for a bright red strawberry at the top the bunch.

Castan's face went instantly hard again, and he all but slapped the berry out of Bridle's hand. "That isn't for you."

"I brought it for everyone," Euphy tried to clarify, setting it on the table.

"Even so, Golden is our leader, which means he's the official host, and we have to respect rank around here." Castan looked at Bridle. "Golden gets first pick. You can have what he chooses not to take."

Euphy saw a streak of pink flash across Bridle's cheeks, and heard him mutter, "Some leader, who can't even pay attention to his job."

Castan heard, too.

"Excuse me?"

Bridle, emboldened now that he'd been caught, looked square at Castan and said "I'd bet he couldn't tell you even five of our squadrons' names, or what any of them do. Does he even know that Gioa's manning the gate right now, or that Serena raced a mounted peace officer on foot yesterday, just to see whether she could, and she nearly matched it? But you're telling me that I, the one who thinks about these things every day, am less worthy than someone who's not in a place to know or care about any of that?"

"Yes, I am telling you that."

"Then think of me as testing this for poison, if it makes you feel better," retorted Bridle, his mouth twisting down as he grabbed the berries, almost knocking the whole bag over as he turned and stormed out of the tent.

So maybe all the meetings *did* end like this.

Euphy slipped out of the tent, unsure of what he ought to say to the furious Castan, but not wanting to look like he was bolting away as fast as he could (which he was).

The difference between the heat of the tent and the crisp, quiet air outside was immediately noticeable. Euphy took a deep breath, feeling his head clear a little.

But Bridle didn't seem to be refreshed by the cool breeze. He stood with his arms crossed, gazing moodily at the water. How different he looked from the companionable, gentle-faced young man in the market that morning.

When Euphy joined him on the bank, Bridle immediately sighed. "Sometimes I just can't take it, you know? It's my job to strategize, and Castan thinks I shouldn't be allowed to do it, though it's what *he* agreed to when they brought me on. I'd love to leave him to his own ways, and let him see how far he gets."

He bent and picked up a stone, then tossed it across the water. It didn't even skip; it just sank.

"It's not that I don't like Golden, or that I don't think he ought to be our king. I do. I really believe all of that. But I *don't* think he's capable of taking the crown right now.

I mean, we've got to be practical here. If I were as distracted as that, Castan would send me packing, and with good reason. If Golden can't even pay attention in our Command Room, how is he going to lead us when the actual battle comes?

A bustle of movement came from the right, and they turned to see Castan rumbling toward them.

"Oh, brother. Here we go," Bridle groaned, but he held his head up gallantly in the face of Castan's wrath, and did not back down when Castan demanded of him, "Just what do you think you're about, young man?"

"I'm about my own business, and I came out here to mind it. You're the one who's stirring up trouble again."

"If you care so little about Golden, why don't you leave?"

"It's because I *do* care that I'm saying these things. What good did allowing someone to stay comfortable forever in their self-pity do for them when they were trying to achieve something?"

"He's already done more than you have," Castan retorted. "He's faced Livio once – the only one who tried it and survived."

"But pining for the good old days isn't going to win us any battles *now*. He might have been the only one capable of fighting Livio back then, but do you really think he could do it right now? We either need to find a way to push him forward, or start looking for someone who doesn't need that push."

"Don't you see? That's – " Castan stopped with a strangled sound. Bridle had, knowingly or not, hit the very thing which was eating Golden away, one day a time: The knowledge that he was different than who he used to be, that he seemed to have regressed to a level below even where he'd been as a young man, and could not find the way to catch up to where he ought to be by now.

Every one of the morrismen had seen Golden's forlorn tendencies on display, but none of them had seen Golden the way he'd been Castan had first met him. None had seen just how empty and paralyzed he had been back then.

Where he was now was progress from that point, however small. Or that was what Castan told himself.

Once he and Golden had started forming their forces, gathering others around them who viewed Livio as they did, and who shared their opinion about what needed to happen to his throne, Castan had thought he might gain some help in bringing Golden back to himself, but that expectation was hard to hold onto when met with words like those which Bridle didn't hesitate to speak.

It was easy to see that Golden still had a long way to go before he was whole again, and it easy to criticize him for it. But how many of the others were actually fighting the battle to help him get there? They might physically help him take his throne, but could they help him be ready for it in his heart? How many of them could do what Castan had done, sheltering the broken prince, taking him by the hand, at times carrying him along, to help him find his way through the miasma that ever hung in front of him?

And how could Castan admit any of these things in front of such a callous youth? Bridle's opinion of Golden was already low enough. For him to know what their leader had been like, and still was like on particularly dark days when no one but Castan was watching, would likely sink it further.

He'd fought the battle for Golden's mind by himself for this long; he supposed he could keep on fighting it a little longer.

CHAPTER 12
In the Fields of Frost and Snow

Euphy found himself being escorted away by the other man who'd been in the Command Room, and who introduced himself in quiet tones as Emmanuel.

"Since it seems like we'll have to skip the meeting tonight, I'd better fill you in on where we are, and where we're trying to get to."

He told Euphy how he and the woman who had been with him, whose name was Vitalia, served as captains of Vanya's forces alongside Bridle and Castan. Each of them were in turn aided by lieutenants, who were also supposed to attend the Command Rooms, on those nights when the meetings were actually able to be held.

Euphy liked his serious, thoughtful way of speaking, and how he was the first person Euphy had met in this camp so far who didn't wear every emotion on his sleeve (and Euphy could admit that this included himself). Vanya was going to need that kind of person if he became king, because Bridle and Castan were probably not going to be able to counsel him rationally if tonight was any indication.

Dandy was another person like Emmanuel, but after that night, Bridle flatly refused to raise the issue with Castan himself, and Euphy hesitated to ask Vanya for fear of sounding insensitive, as if they were devaluing or replacing him – a thought which wouldn't do anything beneficial for his emotional state.

In the end, they decided to ask Emmanuel and Vitalia. Both of them, along with their lieutenants, took their turns meeting Dandy in the market, and both came away recommending him to Castan.

At their urging, Castan consented to meet with him, though he wasn't satisfied with just a single meeting. He'd had a lot of practice in determining the trustworthiness of those who said they opposed Livio, and in his conversations with Dandy, he would drop casual references to names from the past, would make ambiguous statements about Livio that could be taken as aversion by a sympathetic listener, but could just as easily be explained away as neutral to a someone who supported the current king.

"How did you come to work in the castle?" he asked in a tone that impressed Euphy with how well he masked his usual gruffness.

"The lady I serve chose me herself."

"And what sort of lady is she? Does she care much about the courtly life?" asked Castan, which meant that he wanted to know how much she subscribed to Livio's ways.

But Dandy was no less skilled at saying what he meant without saying it outright. "Not at all," he answered. "She has no love for the sort of things the other courtiers enjoy."

"Well, it's true that parties aren't for everyone. Is there nothing else she likes to do? No one she cares to talk to, or anything she cares to talk about?"

"Only me, really, beside her lady's maid. And we don't talk about what goes on in the rest of the palace."

"If she finds nothing to suit her there, why does she stay? Has she considered leaving?"

"Ah, you see – " said Dandy. "She's something of an invalid. She wouldn't be able to support herself without Livio's assistance. But I make sure she doesn't run into too much trouble – that she doesn't have to deal with anything which isn't suited to her tastes."

The conversation carried on like this, with each of them watching the other carefully to see how they would take each question and answer. Castan must have been pleased with what he saw, for he eventually posed the clearest question he had yet.

"Euphemio's told me that you've said you wished you had been in the castle when Nereus was alive. That you wished you could have done something to save him. Did you really mean that? If someone challenged Livio someday, the way he challenged Nereus, what would you do?"

"I think I would have to help them. So many people were hurt – *are* being hurt – by what happened, and all for what? Power? Greed? If I had a chance to put things to right, I would have to take it."

The pride and conviction in his answer seemed to be enough for Castan, and it wasn't long afterwards that he told Euphy to bring Dandy for a first visit to the camp. It wasn't long after *that* before Dandy was invited to join the Command Room, though Castan stipulated that Dandy was not to see or even know of Vanya's existence until even further observation could be made of him.

Castan had been forced to admit many people to their group since the day he'd met the prince, otherwise they would never have gathered enough forces to do anything like taking the kingdom back, but none of those save Euphemio had met their real leader without another prolonged period of scrutiny from Castan first. Those who did meet him were introduced to him as just another dancer long before they were told of his real identity.

Euphy had been the one exception to this rule, and that was because Golden himself had decided it. But Castan was not going to let that happen again, especially so soon after the last time.

And so to protect their prince, Dandy was kept from knowing about Golden in any respect. The morrismen let Dandy think Castan was the one in charge, which wasn't hard to do, given how he issued orders and opinions enough to make anyone believe that were the case. They even went so far as to have Tobiah, Castan's lieutenant, pose as "Golden" in the Command Room, so that they could freely discuss their tactics without modification.

This meant that Golden no longer attended the meetings himself, and that Castan, Bridle, Vitalia, and Emmanuel, along with Tobiah, had to brief him on each night's proceedings afterwards. Bridle argued that staying away from the action wasn't helping Golden grow into the leader he needed to be, and that it was creating more work than was necessary for themselves. But Castan declared that it was good practice to ensure that they understood the plan well enough to repeat it.

"And who are we going to tell Dandy we intend to put on the throne?" Bridle asked.

"We'll tell him it'll be a republic. You ought to like that, since you're the one who loves to fuss about everyone – namely yourself – getting their piece heard."

"A mind like his would see through that in a minute. He'll be able to tell there's no solid plan there."

"Then use that strategic mind of *yours* that you're always on about and come up with a plan that would work. We'll give that to him."

Through Bridle bristled at having to spend so much effort on a task which was ultimately pointless, he was thrilled from the start with Dandy himself. As he'd said on the day in Clockface Market, having someone dashing and decisive with them made him feel as if they were actually starting to move forward.

It didn't hurt that Dandy tended to agree with Bridle's points in the meetings., and when it was the authoritative, experienced Dandy arguing the issues, rather than "that troublesome Bishop", Castan tended to agree with them, too.

Euphy felt a bit sorry for Bridle, thinking that it must hurt to have his own points ignored just because he was the one who said them, while the very same ideas were accepted when they came from someone else.

"Are you joking? It's great!" Bridle exclaimed. "I'm happy if anyone can get the old crank to see reason. I don't care if it's me who does it or not."

But while Bridle was nothing but pleased with Dandy's contributions, there was something within Euphy that wasn't entirely comfortable with the way things had been going since Dandy had joined them.

Many of the morrismen were flocking to Dandy, eager to hear what someone who worked directly with the nobles might share. This wouldn't have bothered Euphy on its own, as he himself often went to Dandy for information. But it seemed Dandy was acting differently in this environment than he did in the palace.

Being surrounded by people who adored him seemed to be puffing him up, and making him behave less like a friendly older brother and more like a condescending one who saw no sin in exercising his privileges over someone beneath him.

When Euphy would put forth a comment in the Command Room, Dandy had developed a habit of drawing attention to anything he found silly in it, of making a barbed remark – sometimes veiled behind humor, sometimes not – saying things like "Forgive me, Euphy, but if you had trouble finding your way through a library, you'll agree that you probably wouldn't know the best way to maneuver through a battlefield."

Dandy might have had a point, but Euphy didn't see why he had to bring it up in front of everyone, or why nobody else noticed how hurtful his response was. But then, the strength of Dandy's opinions was what had merited his invitation to the camp in the first place. So why should anybody ask him to be any different?

Once, Euphy had arrived slightly later than normal to camp. There had been a line for the usual fruits and treats which he'd gotten into the habit of bringing, and by the time he got to the Command Room, he found Dandy there with papers and maps already spread over the table, with stones to mark potential movements on a battlefield scattered across them.

Dandy took one look at the basket on Euphy's arm, and without a single word of greeting, said "Just take that somewhere else. I have no room for it here."

Euphy didn't even bother to respond. For one thing, he wasn't stupid, and it wasn't as if he would have tried to set the thing down on top of Dandy's papers. But what bothered him most of all was the fact that, in Dandy's eyes, Euphy wasn't even worth the effort of saying "hello" to. He wasn't even as important as Dandy's being able to have his table arranged just right.

Euphy wanted to believe that Dandy really wasn't aware of how he was behaving. He wanted to view Dandy sympathetically, but it was getting difficult to do when Dandy would not view *him* sympathetically.

Though even with all this going on, Euphy found he was able to bear it thanks to fact that he had Minari to turn to.

Contrary to how he'd felt even just a few weeks ago, the stone pen had turned into the most comfortable place he knew, the spot where he could speak most freely.

Since the day when Euphy had first brought the fresh food to Minari, he'd felt that he could speak about what was on his mind when they were together. The old tension between them had dissipated, and once he started talking, he found that he almost could not stop. He shared amusing stories from the staff hall, interesting things he had seen in the market, and anything else that might make the unicorn feel less trapped.

On Minari's side, the sharp commands and terse answers he'd been used to giving Euphy transformed into amiable commentary and even advice.

It was strange and wonderful to hear the ethereal voice speak on sometimes commonplace matters, but even that now sounded elevated when communicated by a unicorn's tongue.

True, Minari still looked at him with those bright, fathomless eyes, evaluating everything he said. But that meant he was paying attention, which was more than could be said for Dandy, and though they sometimes disagreed, Minari didn't mock or dismiss Euphy's ideas the way Dandy did.

Funny how this creature, who used to inspire fear and astonishment in him, was now his place of refuge; the one with whom he shared things he couldn't tell anyone else.

Minari even allowed him to lean close one day and whisper to him the truth of the morrismen and the goal they had of overthrowing Livio. And though this was something that even they couldn't speak openly about for fear of the skulking hunters overhearing, they could talk about struggles Euphy faced in the camp as long as they were careful not to say anything too detailed aloud.

"Thoughtlessness toward others is often born of an overabundance of worry regarding one's own situation," Minari said when Euphy had explained the issue with Dandy, though he hadn't named Dandy directly.

"Perhaps your friend's own troubles are so consuming that he hasn't the strength left to notice anyone else's. You might ask him about his own concerns someday."

"Oh, trust me, there is no shortage of people who want to hear his thoughts."

"But do any of them want to hear his personal cares? Or are they all concerned with what he can do for them? If you can help him unburden himself of some of them, he might then have enough room in his heart to pay attention to yours."

"Maybe I would ask him if he'd ever let me get a decent word in," Euphy pouted.

"Do," said Minari simply, and Euphy felt better for the fact that he hadn't commented on his bit of petulance.

"Speaking of troubles," said Euphy, reminded of someone else. "What would you do if you knew someone who used to be…used to be cheerful and brave…but he's had a lot of troubles since then, and he wasn't able to do all the things he wanted to? And now he feels like he can't do anything useful at all. He thinks he's missed his chances, and he spends a lot of his time wishing he could back and redo them.

He's one person I *have* spent a lot of time listening to, but I don't really know what to say to him. What would *you* say to him?"

Minari looked at him for several second without speaking.

"I guess an immortal like yourself wouldn't see what was so hard about his situation," Euphy said, and Minari nickered in that laughing way of his.

"We are not immortal," he said. "I suppose we seem so compared to you, but we do age. What puzzles me is that you humans would sorrow over the marks of time in yourselves, when you admire it so in our race."

Euphy took his own turn at being puzzled. "I don't think I follow."

"Do you know," explained Minari, "that humans always say unicorns are disappearing? You say there are so few unicorns left in the world now, when people a hundred years before you said exactly the same.

It is not that we disappear. When we are born, and we are young and foolish, we are invisible to humans. Your eyes cannot see the color we are then. Once we grow older and gain wisdom, that is when we become white, and many are so foolish that they either never grow old enough to become white, or else they grow older without growing wiser, and thus remain invisible. There are enough unicorns in the world. But not all of us gain enough experience to deserve a white coat. It is not something to be lamented.

86

It is the same with humans. Your hair grows white as you grow in wisdom, but what you find so beautiful in unicorns, you dread to see in yourselves."

"But if you're old enough that your coat is white now, does that mean you're going to die soon?" Euphy asked, feeling a sudden constriction in his throat.

"Not unless something were to harm me from without." He looked down at the chains on his feathered feet.

"Then the way you look isn't really beautiful. It does you harm – makes you visible to people who would hurt you, like Livio."

"It can't be helped. That is the danger that comes with living, and I would refuse to do the alternative, to retain the color of youth and foolishness."

Euphy had a feeling that wasn't what Minari would have said just a few weeks ago. But he supposed this proved Minari's earlier point: Having someone go to the trouble of understanding your burdens could make all the difference. It had clearly worked even for a unicorn. Why couldn't it work on Dandy as well?

CHAPTER 13
The Pool of Narcissus

"I'm sorry, but I haven't been able to find anything about what your brother's name meant," Dandy admitted to Theodora. "Do you have any other ideas? Any other information I can go on? I know you were eager to remember it."

"Was I? I didn't know it meant anything in the first place. How did you know?" she asked, but then answered her own question. "Well, I'm not surprised. You know so much more than I do."

She showed no sign of being concerned over having gone from not knowing the meaning of her brother's name to not knowing that it had a meaning at all, or that she had ever told Dandy about it.

It wasn't the first time she had forgotten that she'd told him things. But the way she was so utterly untroubled by it this time was concerning. Before, she would notice when she couldn't recall something about her family.

"I wish I could remember more about him," she had said when she'd first told him of her brother's name. But now, such a desire was replaced by her pleasant, obliging laugh, which in this particular instance did not feel so pleasant.

She was getting worse. Dandy had waited all these years, and she'd never improved, which was fine when Livio was frittering his time away on other things, and there was relative peace around them. But now that things were moving, when Livio and the rebels were both consolidating their power, and there was a chance of another upheaval, it was crucial that she have some protection, some means of defending herself.

The previous overthrow had shocked her so much that it had turned her into the shell he saw before him. What might another one do? He had to find some way to heal her before then.

He wished he could warn her of what was coming. But if he did that, she might unthinkingly repeat his words to anyone without knowing what she did.

He briefly considered asking Castan's advice on the situation, but it wasn't something he could share with Castan either, unless he wanted to give away what job he really did in the palace. He'd convinced them all so far that he was simply a Ausonian servant paid to attend upon an Albionite courtier, rather than an Albionite courtier himself, whose job, if he was being honest, was really more like a jailer to an Ausonian one.

So getting the opinion of any of the morrismen was not an option. What other choices were there? Anyone from inside the court would doubtless question why Dandy was so interested in restoring the memories of a former enemy princess. As it was, she was only allowed to stay in the palace because she could not remember that she was their enemy.

Dandy thought again. Where else could he go?

Livio believed that unicorns had all kinds of powers, and that they could transfer those powers to humans, or at least use them in favor of humans. That was why he had wanted to capture one in the first place. Was the ability to heal among those powers? And would the unicorn in the dungeon be willing to heal Theodora?

But how could he make such a thing happen? How did one convince a unicorn to do you a favor? Even Livio didn't know that part yet, which was why the creature continued to dwell below the castle, the mysterious beast beneath all of their feet, but which few people had seen, and nobody really knew anything about, except possibly the grooms who dwelt in the depths beside it.

It struck Dandy then: Euphy was a groom. He might be just the person who could persuade it to heal Theodora, its fellow captive.

Dandy had seen the creature once, from a distance, on the day when he had taken Theodora's horse out to the plaza. Euphy had not been in the stable that day, and Dario, who had saddled and brought Rusciu to him, had quickly shooed him out when he noticed Dandy eyeing the pen in the recesses behind the horse stalls.

But Euphy, as a friend, ought to let him get closer than that.

When Dandy arrived at the stable, he found Euphy perched on a low stool. His head was bent over a water bucket which he was scrubbing out, and he didn't see Dandy approaching.

When he did notice Dandy, his face settled into a tired look of recognition.

Euphy, for his part, had wanted to do what Minari had suggested, and to try and be a friendly ear to Dandy, but he was caught off-guard by seeing the man appear here, in the one place that remained to Euphy which was free of his influence. But telling himself that Minari would be proud of him if he tried, Euphy forced his face into a normal expression and said, "What's going on? You need me to get Rusciu ready for you?"

"No, thanks," said Dandy. "I'm not going out just now. I simply thought I'd come to see what you do during the day," Dandy said, aware of how false his chipper tone must sound. But he had to do it. He had no wish to explain more about Theodora and risk exposing the half-truths he had let the rebels believe.

Euphy bent over his bucket again so that Dandy wouldn't see the annoyance creeping onto his face.

"*Looking for something **else** to criticize me about, maybe*," he thought, but made an effort to stop himself. He looked toward Minari's pen, trying to draw strength from him, to remind himself of what the better course of action would be. But his gaze lingered too long, and Dandy followed it.

"So that's what Livio's relying on to make him a king forever," Dandy said, still trying to sound nonchalant as he continued. "Do you know what it's supposed to do for him? How it can help him?"

"You'd probably know that more about that than I would. What with your inside knowledge from working in the court and all," Euphy said, not looking up. He was reproaching himself for having drawn Dandy's attention to Minari, not knowing Dandy had already had the subject in mind.

When Euphy didn't offer anything more, Dandy took a breath and ventured to introduce his point into the silence. "I wonder whether a unicorn would be willing to help someone who had a real necessity, rather than someone who was just looking to take advantage of it."

"You mean someone like you? You think you have a real need?" Euphy asked curtly. His resolve to be polite was evaporating with the advancing realization of what Dandy had really come here for.

"It isn't my need, exactly. To start with, I'd just like to know whether it might be willing to listen if I talked with it."

"*Of course*," thought Euphy. So it wasn't enough for Dandy to be superior in every other aspect. He had to come here, to the one place that Euphy could escape him, and exert his superiority in dealing with Minari, too.

"Why don't you try it?" Euphy tossed the question out, knowing full well that Dandy would be unable to do any such thing. Let this man who fancied himself so important see what it felt like to be humbled before someone more

92

powerful than himself. He watched Dandy approach Minari, smirking as he saw how tentatively Dandy stepped.

As Euphy had known he would be, Minari was in a fine temper at seeing a stranger approach, and had no intention of letting anyone get close to himself. He tossed his head and trumpeted so loudly that Dandy threw his hands over his ears. Even Euphy was forced to cover his own ears at the sound, and he had already known it was coming.

He was pleased at how startled and unsure Dandy looked, especially considering that this wasn't even as loud as Minari could be. He had been louder on that first night, when he was healthier, and the wild forest air was still in his lungs.

But the noise was enough to make Dandy reconsider getting close to him, much less attempting to speak to him. He backed away, not knowing what words of farewell he said to Euphy, and tried not to stumble on his way out of the stable, feeling that he wouldn't be able to draw a full breath until he were out of that dark oppressive place where the power of the creature was built up between the heavy stone walls, with no outlet for it to escape.

When he reached the door which led back up to the castle, he looked over his shoulder at Euphy. Now that the unicorn had stopped its bone-rattling cry, Euphy had entered its pen, and seemed to be speaking words of comfort to it. Even he did not touch it, but the stamping of the shining hooves was less fierce now, and it lowered its proud head a little, to be closer to Euphy's level.

A rivulet of something like jealousy twinged through Dandy at the sight. He had thought that if he could bring Theodora here, the unicorn would heal her. But if his own head was spinning after an encounter of just a few moments, what would that do to Theodora's fractured mind?

Wasn't there any way for another person to get as close to it as Euphy was? Euphy, by all indications, had learned to handle that oppressively magnificent aura, but unless

Dandy could spend all of his days mucking out its stall, he didn't see how gaining a relationship like that was possible.

For one thing, even if he wanted to do that, Livio would likely have something to say about it. And the unicorn would have even more to say about it, if today was anything to go by.

Turning the problem over in his mind, Dandy thought that in place of asking the unicorn directly, perhaps he could convince Euphy to ask it in his place. If he were as close to it as he looked just now, would the unicorn refuse him?

He'd have a better chance to ask again in the evening. Euphy might be distracted with work and the unicorn's presence during the day, but at night, amongst the morrismen, maybe he'd be more disposed to listen. And if not, Dandy could get the others to back him, and convince Euphy of the necessity.

Already the sting of the unicorn's rejection was fading as he saw visions of Theodora coming to herself again, just in time for the removal of Livio. Not all was lost for her yet.

That night, when the usual disagreement over the best course of action broke out among the morrismen, Dandy saw his chance.

"I have to tell you that Livio has a weapon which he intends to use to make himself more powerful than he's ever been. If he can do it, then it's likely that none of what we plan here will matter at all. But I say we should take that secret weapon for ourselves. If it's something that can make a king, it can unmake one as well."

On the other side of the tent, Euphy felt his blood running colder with each word. He stared at Dandy, horrified at what he was about to reveal.

Dandy spoke with all the beneficence of a prophet revealing the blessings of Heaven to mere mankind, but to Euphy, his words sounded more like a curse declaring Minari's doom.

Worse yet was the fact that, through the ringing in his stunned ears, Euphy managed to make out his own name being spoken by that terrible voice.

"Euphy can confirm the truth of it. He cares for the animal, very carefully, from what I've seen."

Weeks Dandy had spent dismissing, ignoring, and silencing Euphy, and *now* he called on Euphy to speak? Now when it was convenient for Dandy, never mind what it would do to anyone else? Never mind how it would put Minari at risk if everyone knew about him and about the power he was said to give? No, Dandy apparently only cared about what *he* wanted.

"He's not something to be used," Euphy protested, but if anyone listened to what he said, he wasn't aware of it. They were all so caught up in the grandness of Dandy's idea, and none of them knew exactly what it was they were supporting.

He could see how, from the outside, using Minari sounded like a good plan. He well remembered his own struggle over whether to tell the morrismen about Minari himself. But all he had meant was to warn them about what Livio intended to do, not suggest that they take Minari's power instead.

And just what was Dandy planning to do to get a hold of that power anyway? Was that why he had come to the stable earlier? To try and slither his way into Minari's trust just so that he could turn around and trade him to the morrismen in exchange for being adored as their savior? How was this any different than Livio using Minari to gain power and prestige for himself?

Euphy turned and pushed his way out of the tent. He had to appeal to Vanya. Vanya knew what it was like to try to save someone else when you didn't have the strength to save yourself.

But when Euphy told him the story, he saw Vanya's expression brighten at the prospect in the moments before Euphy explained his reasons for opposing it.

"Of course you're right. We ought not use a living thing for our own gain without its permission," he said, and the wistfulness which settled back onto him was painful to witness after that moment when he had looked almost himself again.

Instead of relief, Euphy had found another burden to carry. He absolutely could not allow Minari to be used as an object of warfare against his will. Not even for Vanya. But he wished he *could* find something to bring that look to the prince's face once more. He'd managed to help Minari emerge from his heartsickness, but was there any way to save Vanya along with him, without sacrificing Minari again?

He knew that if he did nothing, Minari would still have to fall eventually. The truth was that these pleasant days with him could not last. Euphy might have restored his health, but he could not ultimately undo the chains around him. He didn't even know where the key to them was, if it existed at all. He doubted Livio would have made any provisions for Minari to get out of the dungeon alive, so it was possible that there wasn't one.

It was a fact that he'd been dimly aware of in the back of his mind, but he'd been able to avoid thinking of it until now, when it had been so harshly illuminated by Dandy's selfishness and Vanya's hopelessness.

He would need a force greater and stronger than himself to free Minari, a force capable of completely removing Livio as a threat at all. Vanya was the only one who had a chance at that, and Minari's power, however it was supposed to be gotten, was the only thing that could make him capable of doing so.

However selfish Dandy's motives were for saying it, he had been right. Vanya and the morrismen did need Minari. And Euphy would need to step out of the way.

The coldly bright vision of how it would be flooded his mind. Minari would shake off his chains and the darkness of his days in the dungeon as the shining prince and the glorious unicorn freed each other, and they would triumphantly march to the reclaimed throne. The celebration and rejoicing would be great, but there would be no place for Euphy there even if someone did remember to invite him. He had no knowledge of what it took to run a kingdom, like Vanya did. Nor did he have any particular power to aid in running it, as Minari did.

The two of them belonged at such heights, and Euphy could not follow them. They would go on to glory and renown, restoring the country and being rightly venerated. No one would remember the lowly stablehand who had cared and sacrificed for them both.

Euphy would remain down below in the muck while the ones he loved moved on without him. It was an awful feeling, but letting them free each other was the only way to save them, and it no longer mattered what Euphy felt about it.

"What's the matter? You look like someone's died," said a voice – Dandy's voice – as Euphy found himself wandering through the camp after bidding goodbye to Vanya. Dandy must have seen how Euphy was one of the few in the whole area who was not excitedly chattering over the new prospective advantage in the war against Livio and Albion.

How unexpected that he, of all people – the one who had incited the night's terrible revelations in the first place, who had shown Euphy that his own thoughts on the issue didn't matter unless they could serve the larger purpose – would be the one to notice his feelings now.

Euphy's first inclination was to tell Dandy to leave him alone, but Minari's words still hadn't stopped echoing in his head, about how sharing troubles could help lighten their weight. Maybe he and Dandy could still find some common ground after everything that had happened.

Given that his remaining time together was short, this might be one of the last things Euphy could do to please him. He wanted the last memories with Minari to be happy ones.

"I just…" he started, hearing his own voice quake, and then he was all at once pouring out his fears for the future, his concern for Minari's well-being no matter who tried using his power, his own dread of being left behind.

He looked at Dandy, almost breathless from the confession, and felt his heart hanging in the balance. To have poured out all of those feelings was a difficult thing, but he had to trust that Minari was right. That the sharing of feelings would make Dandy remember the sympathy he'd once possessed. That he would not laugh at or dismiss them.

What Dandy actually did was worse. With a lightning flash of emotion that twisted his face into snarl, he snapped at Euphy, "What a selfish notion. You admit that so many other people would be helped by the unicorn, but you're choosing to think only of yourself. I would be ashamed to be so self-indulgent as to consider withholding such a gift for the sake of my own ego."

The words fell on Euphy like a hailstorm.

"You think your wishes should be paramount over everything else. That you alone should be allowed the privilege of being close to the unicorn."

"That's not what I – "

It was because Euphy had known that he must give Minari up that he had said anything to Dandy in the first place. If he had really wanted to keep them to himself, it would have been as easy as ceasing to advise the morrismen on how to overthrow Livio. But he'd committed to their cause, even knowing that it take his own dreams away from him.

"Whether you intended it or not, your saying something like that shows what's really in your heart," Dandy continued, unrelenting. "You're betraying all of us by being so contrary to what would be best for the most people."

By this time, Euphy's eyes were stinging. Dandy had claimed to know what was in Euphy's heart, but he didn't care enough to actually look into it, or to to provide any real comfort. He never had. He only cared enough to make it *look* like he did.

It was easy enough to teach someone how to use a simple library card, or to offer silver compliments about how well they cared for stupid horses, then to bask in the admiration that these low-effort actions earned him.

It was another thing entirely to take the time to understand the baring of someone's soul, which would require Dandy to give something of himself without gaining anything in return.

This, then, was why Dandy had begun to treat Euphy so coldly after joining the morrismen. Because Euphy did not fawn over him the way the others did. He did not always defer to his judgement, or expect Dandy to tell him what to think.

And it was evident that Dandy would have no one near him who did not set him up as the most important being in their lives. All Euphy had been to him was one more subject to adore him, and when Euphy no longer played that part, Dandy no longer had a use for him.

"Have you finished complaining, or am I expected to watch you mope, too?" Dandy asked. "You're not the only person I have to speak to, you know."

Euphy looked away, willing his tears not to fall. These feelings were his entire world, and to Dandy, they were nothing more than an inconvenience.

"I'd have expected better of you, Euphy," muttered Dandy, with a wounded tone that clearly communicated which of the two of them he considered the victim, then turned away, not seeing or choosing not to see Euphy's own stricken face.

Euphy let him go, and stumbled past the camp's perimeter without a word to anyone else. He dimly remembered Lazaro, on the night watch again, looking at him in concern, but he didn't stop until he was alone in the field, and lingered, shivering in the autumn cold for as long as he could, to avoid having to meet Dandy again on the path back to Prisma.

Prior to tonight, they had sometimes walked together, but looking back at it, that was probably just another of Dandy's false kindnesses – which he displayed if the other person was acting according to what *he* considered right. If it was a situation where their opinions or desires differed from Dandy's, then that person would be made to see that Dandy's view was *always* the right view, his way *always* the right way.

That must have been why he'd accused Euphy of thinking only of his own wishes. Because thinking of his own wishes was what *Dandy* was used to doing. For someone used to demanding their own way, it must have been galling to think that anyone else might try to ask for theirs instead.

It wasn't that Dandy thought anyone else's purposes were less important than his own. It was that no one else ought to have any goals or wishes at all, outside of those prescribed to them by Dandy himself. He had grown so angry at Euphy because that was what one did with an object that wouldn't do what it was made for. To Dandy, Euphy's purpose was to act as a gateway to Minari. He had no more right to refuse Dandy than any object had to refuse to be used by him.

Euphy saw it all now so clearly. All the mystery behind Dandy's changing personality, how he could go from being so excessively kind to so excessively cruel. His kindness was there to draw people to him, to make them love him so that they would be willing to do his bidding when asked. His cruelty was there to punish them if they didn't.

But Euphy discovered that knowing the reasons behind Dandy's behavior didn't stop it from having its intended effect.

To be called selfish when he was trying his best not to be. To be accused of demanding his own way when his heart was breaking from the knowledge that he *would* let his own desires go if he had to. It was disheartening to find that his best efforts were being twisted by Dandy's distorted view into the very things he had worked so hard for them *not* to be.

Was there anyone who would appreciate Euphy for the person he really was? Anyone he could tell his troubles to? Vanya believed he was someone "with the potential to become quality", but Vanya had enough troubles of his own, and after tonight, Euphy knew he couldn't saddle him down with more.

Bridle might have been sympathetic, but Dandy's presence had made things easier for him with Castan, and would it be right for Euphy to take that away? If Euphy exposed Dandy for what he was – a cruel and manipulative man under all of his brilliance – Bridle would lose a hero and a champion.

And how could he tell Minari about any of this? How could he look him in the face and share the fact that he'd had the most awful row over what was Minari's best chance at freedom?

What if Minari turned on him the same way Dandy did? What if the knowledge that Euphy held even a shred of a doubt over something that could free him was enough to erase the bond they had scratched out between them? What if that bond had only formed because Minari had no other choice? Would he be willing to forget it as soon as a better option came along? What if Euphy had been mistakenly

101

cherishing something that meant as little to Minari as it did to Dandy?

When he reached the stable, the last one in from the lonely night, he went about his tasks silently save for the increasingly frequent sniffles which he explained away to Dario as having caught a cold. He said the same to Minari before he could even be asked about it, thus avoiding having to give a truthful answer, as he was always compelled to do when Minari asked him anything.

And when every creature in the dungeon aside from Euphy was asleep, he crept to the pen to gaze on the faintly glowing figure inside, trying to fill up his eyes and his mind with this precious image while it remained to him.

He felt himself reaching for his keys, turning the lock and pushing open the gate as quietly as he could, which was difficult considering the size and weight of a gate that could hold a unicorn, but he got through it without waking Minari, and dropped down, burying his face in the clean hay which he had laid there just that evening. It was scratchy, but at least it muffled the sound of his weeping.

There, next to the white fire which had frightened and confused him once upon a time, was the one place left in the world where he could find any comfort, swiftly-ending comfort though it was.

On that day when Dandy was at the right hand of Vanya's throne, with Minari behind them, would he appreciate the blessing it was to have the unicorn close by? Or would he devalue Minari as he did everyone else – as a mere means to an end?

But the cold truth was that it didn't really matter. Being devalued by Dandy would still be better for him than staying here. Here, he would fade again eventually, no matter how much Euphy appreciated him. A unicorn could not stay trapped in a stone dungeon forever. Euphy wished the same could be said for himself.

CHAPTER 14
The Fey King

He woke to the sound of trumpeting, and Minari towering above him, tossing his head.

Euphy's chest seized in panic as he recalled where he was. He rolled as far away from the restless hooves as he could and scrambled to his feet. Rushing to the paddock door, he saw Stregatto approaching, who would have found him sleeping there if he had woken any later.

They exchanged the usual unpleasantries as Euphy hurried out of the gate and locked it behind him.

"You've got straw all over you, boy," Stregatto said. "What did you do, sleep in the hay like one of your animals?"

"Does Livio know you're down here?" Euphy asked.

"The *king's* the one who sent me," Stregatto said, emphasizing the title as Euphy had failed to do.

Euphy said nothing as he moved toward the horse stalls.

"Don't you want to know why?" Stregatto pressed, falling into stride beside him.

Euphy spared him an irritated glance, which Stregatto took as an answer, for he went on with what he'd come to say, nodding back toward Minari.

"Seems like you've got some kind of connection to that animal."

"He hasn't killed me yet, at least," Euphy said darkly. He hadn't intended to reply at all, but he was tired, so tired that these people couldn't just leave him alone. Dandy, Dario,

Stregatto – what gave them all the right to badger him like this, anytime they chose?

"Come on, don't be modest," said Stregatto, reaching to pick a piece of straw from Euphy's hair, knowing it would make him flinch. "I've seen times when you sure looked like you were talking with it. The king would love to know about someone with the power to do that – to hear from someone who could tell him about it."

He said it as if it were an offhand remark, but Euphy knew the meaning behind it. He was being summoned.

As if having to deal with a captive unicorn, a melancholy prince, an imperious valet, a critical stablemaster, and a taunting hunter weren't enough, he was now going to have to report to a tyrant king.

Shouldn't this sort of thing have been reserved for those of more consequence than him? Euphy would have thought that a mere stablehand would have had a less eventful path in life. In all the time since the Night of New Glory, neither he nor anyone he knew had been important or powerful enough to be called before Livio.

But then, wasn't it Livio who gave people that power? Wasn't that why the hunters had to be obeyed, even though they didn't belong here – because they had the backing of the king?

A vision filled Euphy's head of what it would feel like to order others around like that. What if, when Dandy said something nasty to him, he could turn around and threaten to report such behavior to the king? What if he could order Stregatto out of the stable any time he came to cause trouble?

A king, bad as he might be, was still a king. And if Euphy was being forced to see him either way, why not make the most of it?

Besides, this wouldn't just help himself. It would be for Vanya and Minari's benefit, too. If they were bound to move forward together, wouldn't having inside information help them? Wouldn't it prove Dandy wrong if Euphy could be the one to give them the very information they needed to leave Euphy behind? How could anyone then accuse him of being selfish?

Euphy raked his hair back with his hand, took a breath, looking straight into Stregatto's glinting eyes.

"Lead the way," he said, steeling himself for wherever that statement might take him.

But Stregatto laughed at his serious face. "You're pretty eager for someone who makes such a show about not wanting us here, though you can't just go to see him whenever you feel like it. You've got wait until he calls you."

"So the king just forgets to make the time for the arrangements he asks for?" Euphy said, trying not to let himself feel foolish. "When exactly does he plan on calling?"

"Patience, boy. I'll let you know," Stregatto flicked him on the ear as he turned to go.

Euphy reflexively reached up to slap his hand away, but Stregatto's reflexes were faster, and his fingers closed around Euphy's wrist, twisting his whole arm down behind his back, into a position that made Euphy feel like either his wrist, his shoulder, or both would pop out of their sockets.

"Try that again and see what happens," Stregatto growled, digging his fingers against the bone before shoving Euphy almost to the ground.

Euphy whipped around, glaring at him but cradling his wrist.

Stregatto leered in return. "I said I would let you know. Try to contain yourself while I'm gone, and don't miss me too much."

"*Once I meet with Livio, let Stregatto try that again and see what happens to **him**,*" thought Euphy when he was alone again with only his stung wrist and stung pride.

Yes, meeting with Livio would definitely be the right thing to do if it could give him to the power to stop all of these bullies, like Dandy and Stregatto both. If he could get the ear of the king, if he could pretend well enough to make Livio think he would get any information out of him, maybe he could also convince Livio to do something for him as the price of that information.

And Stregatto was going to lead him straight to that power. All Euphy had to do was wait.

*　　　*　　　*

It was his first break all day, and he had a terrible ache in his shoulder. An early morning after being woken by a unicorn and manhandled by a hunter could catch up to anyone, but in any case, it had earned him a passing compliment from Dario, who had been happy to see him at work before his usual time.

"Count that as another step in the plan," he said to himself, closing his eyes and leaning against the wall with his good shoulder while trying to stretch out the other.

But he jumped and scraped them both against the stone when Stregatto's voice unexpectedly asked him, "What plan is that?"

His eyes flew open to see the telltale grin as Stregatto announced "The king says he can see you at two o'clock," Euphy twisted his neck to look at the huge clock which Dario kept on the stable wall – the one which he insisted they live and die by.

"That's fifteen minutes from now," Euphy said. He'd counted on having more time to prepare.

"You're free not to come, but I wouldn't want to be you when Livio finds out you refused him. But if you're not a coward – or an idiot – follow me."

"You'll probably lead me into some forgotten corner and leave me there."

The hunter peered around. "You're in one already."

Well, that was true. And then there was the fact that Livio *had* actually bothered to make time for him so quickly.

Euphy had assumed that he would find something more important to do, and shuffle Euphy off to some other time – a time that would be convenient, of course, for Livio, regardless of whether it was for Euphy.

But here he was, with Stregatto sauntering ahead of him, leading him up, up through the floors of the palace, higher than top floor of the library, to the hall which housed the throne.

When Stregatto told him "you're on your own from here," and shut the thick throne room door between them, Euphy was pushed into a room with walls formed almost entirely of colorful glass, flooding the space with prisms of light – a feeling very different from what Euphy had expected of the throne room of the Iron Hand. And at the far end of the hall, in a chair that had been worked into creamy, delicate filigree, was a man who looked not like an imposing king, but rather like a piteously bored schoolboy, with his chin on his hand and wearing a pout.

His face transformed when he saw Euphy, as if he'd been rescued from some deeply unpleasant alternative.

Awash in rainbow light, Livio practically shone as he rose from the filigree chair, his carriage stately and his form elegant, with his hair flowing to his shoulders like some noble elven lord.

Not that Euphy had seen an elven lord before, but if he had, he was sure this was what it would have looked like. Because he had also never seen a unicorn before this year, yet he had instantly known one when he saw it.

"So you're Euphemio. I was worried that you wouldn't come! When I heard that you were willing, I told Stregatto that I would clear my schedule, and that he must bring you right away."

The first thing Euphy noted was how well and naturally Livio handled his name. He didn't mispronounce it or comment on it in any way. Having his name treated with respect and dignity happened infrequently enough that it felt like a pleasant novelty.

And then, with his mind on respect, he became conscious that his dirty stable uniform might not be showing the most respect to Livio.

"I'm sorry. I didn't have time to clean up."

"Please don't worry about that. It means you're working hard. I'd be more concerned if you *weren't* dirty But you must tell me about the unicorn. What is he like? Is he doing well?"

How to describe such a being to anyone? And how to explain that Minari would likely be doing much better if he were free – to the very person who had captured him?

"Ah," said Livio, with a gentle, quiet laugh when Euphy didn't respond. "I'm asking too many questions. Dandy always scolds me for that. A 'busybody' is what he calls me, but let's not talk about such unpleasant things," Livio chattered on, but Euphy barely heard the rest of what he said.

He felt as if wind were rushing past his ears. Had Livio said 'Dandy'? As in, the same person who had scolded *him* about Minari?

"Dandy…?" he repeated.

"Oh, excuse me," said Livio apologetically, noting Euphy's distracted expression. "You would probably know him as The Morningstar, or 'General Morning'."

No, Livio was quite wrong about that. Dandy was the name that was well-known to Euphy. It was "General Morning" which was the unfamiliar one, and hearing it from the mouth of Livio himself made it all the stranger.

"Perhaps I'll send him down to you one day. He might benefit from learning what you know. And since he loves to tell me what to do, I'm sure he would jump at the opportunity to share with me what he picks up."

Livio's eyes sparkled at the joke he couldn't know Euphy understood.

The very sound of someone agreeing that Euphy might be wiser than Dandy in any respect was gratifying. And they were definitely speaking of the same Dandy – the one who loved to lecture and scold others. Could there be two Dandy Mornings within the palace, who both acted like that?

"Even if I don't send him, or if he won't go, you must come up and see me again. I'll have to invite him next time, so you two can meet."

Euphy's could just imagine Dandy's face upon seeing him here; his indignation at seeing the very person he'd humiliated into the dust suddenly on the same footing as him, face to face in the king's court.

"I would love to meet him here," Euphy said, perhaps not hearing the sardonic note in his own voice.

"Then I shall do my best to arrange it," said Livio, sounding as if he had no greater pleasure than the chance to arrange something that might make Euphy happy.

He was apparently so focused on making Euphy feel comfortable and welcomed that he forgot to ask further about Minari. For before anymore was said on that subject, Euphy was already receiving a flowery goodbye in which Livio stopped just short of actually bowing to a stablehand.

Euphy was aware that it was his turn to bow and make his exit, but he became conscious that he was missing one vital piece of information. He'd heard vague comments about the rules surrounding how leave was to be taken from royalty, but it was never anything he thought he'd have to know.

"Do I...am I supposed to back out...or...?" he asked haltingly. How mortifying to have to ask a king such a thing. With his face burning, he waited, expecting to hear the same sort of answer which Dandy might give – chastisement, ridicule, condescension.

But Livio's expression softened. "Of course, you couldn't be expected to know. You needn't worry about bowing for now. Please feel free to leave in the same manner you came. Can you find your way to the door?"

Euphy nodded, and passed back through the rivers of light to where Stregatto was waiting for him outside.

"You manage to survive?" the hunter asked, leaning on a pillar and looking at him over folded arms, spurring Euphy to shake himself out of his stupor when he remembered that Stregatto could have told him what he'd needed to know about taking leave, and hadn't.

"I'm here, aren't I? No thanks to you."

"I'm the one who'll get you back downstairs, so I'd watch that mouth if I were you."

Euphy was tempted to take his chances on his own, but he followed.

When he reached the relief of home, and Stregatto had gone, Euphy went straight to his nightstand and pulled *Research in Fantastica* out from the drawer. He had wanted to talk to Minari to relieve his jangled nerves, but he couldn't lie if Minari asked where he had been. So reading the now-familiar tome was the next best thing he could think of.

He flipped through the well-thumbed section on Unicorns, but couldn't make his mind focus on it. He stared blankly at the pages for a few moments, until, on a whim, he turned to the section on Elves, curious if what he found there would look anything like Livio.

True to his guess, the painting he found, titled "Ithilris of Heledfalas" could easily have been Livio in shape and form. The graceful carriage, the noble bearing, and yes, even the flowing hair. But the picture showed a face stern and haughty, nothing like Livio's.

Livio had smiled to see Euphy come, spoken kindly to him while he was there, and regretted to see him go. Could that genteel man really have been Livio the Iron Hand, who had overrun a country in one night, killed all of a royal family, and kept a mighty unicorn as a prisoner?

After all, Dandy had two faces. If he could put on the appearance of goodness, while in reality being "General Morning", couldn't the other have the reputation of cruelty, but really be the one who possessed true kindness?

Couldn't it be the same as Euphy himself, who appeared to be nothing but a stablehand, but had the potential to become quality, as had once been declared by no one less than a prince?

But for the first time since learning of Dandy's identity, Euphy thought of what it would mean for that prince, and the answer froze his blood. If Dandy was part of the morris crew now, and yet was really Livio's underling – that had to mean he was reporting everything he saw and heard straight back to Livio. And genteel or not, no king would take kindly to the knowledge of anyone planning rebellion against him.

Euphy gave a prayer of thanks that Castan had the foresight to keep Vanya's existence a secret, but Dandy could carry everything else back: their plans, their names, every word they'd said.

But if that were the case, why wouldn't Livio have thrown Euphy into prison right away? He'd been right in front of him, and Stregatto would have loved the chance to haul him away in chains, the way he had done to Minari.

Thoughts of princes, elven and otherwise, were soon put to an end by Dario flinging the door to Euphy's room open with a look that said he was, as usual, none too happy about something that Euphy had done.

"Where've you been?" he demanded.

But Euphy, having seen the rainbow halls and the very face of the most powerful man in the kingdom, was himself none too willing to put up with Dario.

"Didn't I finish my work for the morning? Weren't you just complimenting me on having gotten everything done so early?" said Euphy.

111

"Don't take that high and mighty tone with me," Dario tried to scold him, but Euphy answered back with perfect coolness.

"If you really want to know, I've been with the king."

"The *king*? You mean Livio? I'm not in the mood for jokes today," said Dario. "Even if you did want to be around him for some reason, what could he have to say to you?"

"Maybe *I* had something to say to him," said Euphy. "Maybe I've been telling him about you, and everything you say down here, where you think he can't hear you."

Dario's expression jerked, as Euphy had intended, despite the fact that he hadn't really spoken much to Livio at all.

Dario was so indignant about the incident that he was actually driven to mention it to Stregatto later in the day, with the idea of getting him to rebuke Euphy for making up lies about the king.

But although the hunter disliked Euphy, he disliked Dario more, and sensing that an affirmation would bother him, he confirmed Euphy's story, sending Dario into fits of anger which he unleashed on Euphy when Stregatto had left.

"The next time you take it into your head to visit that *pretender* of a king, you had better ask me for permission for first."

"And what will you do if I don't?" Euphy returned. "Sorry, but you're not my highest authority anymore. If Livio wants me, it's him I'll answer to, not you."

Dario's mouth opened and closed, but he said nothing. He *could* say nothing. Euphy was right and they both knew it. In silence, he stalked away, thinking how much Euphy looked like when Stregatto when he was right.

Once Dario was gone and Euphy had space to hear himself think, and he knew that he would have to tend to Minari soon. He'd been avoiding it since his meeting with Livio, for if Minari asked him where he'd been, if that temple-bell voice rang in his head, he wouldn't be able to resist answering, and the game would be up before it had even begun.

But as soon as he entered the pen, he could already tell that Minari had a different question in mind.

"There is something wrong with you beyond a simple cold. You were crying last night."

Euphy's heart melted a little at that. So Minari had noticed, and he'd cared enough to ask about it. Maybe it wouldn't be so bad to tell him, at least part of the reason why.

"You'd probably think it was silly, but —"

"Humans say many silly things. But that doesn't mean I don't care to hear them. I might not have…before. But I find I don't mind so much these days."

"Well…I don't want to be left behind."

"By whom?"

"By you," Euphy said weakly.

Minari bobbed his head in the direction of his chains, then tossed it sideways affectionately so that it butted against Euphy's shoulder.

"You see that I'm not going anywhere."

It was the first time he had spoken of his chains without referencing the idea of getting free of them one day, which concerned Euphy. But this was also the first time Minari had made the first move to touch him, and the warmth of that touch was almost enough to make him forget the misery of the past two days.

Almost.

That this touch happened now, of all times, confirmed to him that the closeness of their relationship was dependent on Minari's being in chains. It was only at this moment, when Minari accepted those chains, that he became willing to openly show affection like this to Euphy.

But with Minari's heavy head on his shoulder, Euphy's dark musings weren't dark enough to keep him from running his fingers through the white mane at last, from stroking the ears that were every bit as soft as they looked.

"You may not be going anywhere now, but you will someday," Euphy said. *"I just hope you'll take me with you."*

The truth was that he didn't know how that could happen in any scenario. Even if there were no Vanya, no morrismen, no throne, and Minari were simply running free in his native wildlands again, how could Euphy realistically go with him? How could a human keep up with a creature like this? It had been hard enough just to learn to stand in his presence while Minari had been hobbled and defeated. How could he possibly do it with Minari at his full power? A prince, like Vanya, might be able to, but it seemed to Euphy that he himself was wasn't really meant to live in the realm where great and wondrous things were encountered. He was good enough to have an insignificant brush with a weak and captive unicorn, but to live alongside one in all of its glory was for people of higher degree than him.

And with this, Euphy's thoughts travelled back to the hall of painted glass. Though Livio had seized the throne there wrongfully, it was exactly because he *had* seized it, that he would be useful to Euphy. Because he hadn't inherited the position, Livio had needed to be strong enough to earn it, to elevate himself to the heights he aimed for.

And if Livio had learned to do it, maybe Euphy could do the same. By watching him, Euphy could learn how to become strong enough to be worthy of his dreams.

CHAPTER 15
Aegis

"So how do we borrow a unicorn's power? Do we just ask it nicely? Is that something you can do, Euphy? And even if it agrees, what can it do while it's chained up? Is the power in the unicorn itself, or does it confer power on the person it's helping?"

Bridle's questions flew at him, but Euphy was busy thinking of the Rainbow Hall, and the information he'd gotten there from Livio.

"I don't know. Maybe Dandy does," he deflected. "He's much closer to the court than I am. I'm sure he's heard lots about what Livio's planning to do to make the unicorn serve him."

Dandy gave a righteously exasperated sigh from across the tent. "Euphy, must you always be so difficult?"

Euphy shrugged, feeling bitter satisfaction in place of the hurt which Dandy's last words to him had inflicted. He would let Dandy play at superiority while he had the chance, for Euphy knew he could topple him any moment he chose.

"You've said yourself how you know so much more than me. Why shouldn't we depend on what you know? Unless all of that was exaggeration?"

He stifled a smile and watched Dandy stiffen in indignation. This self-important man was getting upset over the slightest questioning, yet there were many more awful things Euphy could accuse him of.

He let the conversation continue without him, listening as Dandy shared so much less than what he *actually* knew, and when the meeting was over, Euphy lingered in the camp, knowing Dandy wouldn't be able to resist coming to yell at him.

And when the voice of Dandy barked his name with that familiar expectation of being obeyed, Euphy turned with pride and resentment licking at his heart.

"What are you playing at?" Dandy asked sharply. "We're struggling enough as it is, and intentionally causing doubts and discord isn't going to help any. I know you're sulking over your unicorn, but if you don't want to contribute, then why are you even here?"

"Why are *you,* General Morning?" said Euphy cooly despite the flame in his chest.

He had the satisfaction of seeing Dandy's mouth actually drop open, and he continued, "Did you think Livio wouldn't tell me about what you do for him, just because *you* chose not to?"

Dandy's gaping mouth moved for a few moments before he got any words out.

"Livio…? How did you…?"

"He invited me to come see him. You know he wants to find out more about my unicorn, same as you. And I'm the one who knows the most about the subject. Isn't that right?" Euphy said with a pointed look at the one who'd exploited that very fact in front of the others. "Livio tells me a lot of what he knows, too. Including about the people who report to him."

"There are things…years of history…that you don't understand," Dandy stuttered.

"I understand more than you think."

"But not enough to realize that nothing good can come of dealing with Livio."

"Only if it's *me* doing it, right? Only poor, lowly Euphy has to stay away from him. *You're* allowed to speak to him any time you please."

How could Dandy look down on him for this when *he* was doing the exact same thing? They were equals now in terms of the type of people they associated with.

"That's enough," Dandy cut him off, attempting to take hold of his usual commanding tone again.

"Does Castan know?" Euphy pressed, ignoring him. "Do any of them? Do you know how easy it would be for me to tell them?"

Euphy could spit the truth out in front of everyone and ruin Dandy's credibility on the spot. But it would be much more rewarding to watch him squirm, to see him waiting in fear for the day when Euphy's whim might change and he would reveal the secret of General Morning.

"I could expose you the same way," Dandy tried.

"But, you see, I was a rebel first, and I'm going to Livio so that I can use what I learn from him. You were with Livio long before this. What's your excuse?"

"You must believe me; I don't support him any longer. I really do want to see him overthrown."

"Oh, I believe it. You're good at overthrowing kings," Euphy said, and Dandy winced.

"Besides, you were speaking against him even before you knew anything about the rebellion, and Livio doesn't know anything about us yet, so I believe you haven't told him. But what I can't stand is you acting so high and mighty about doing 'what's right', when you've been nothing but a liar this whole time."

"I haven't had a choice," Dandy argued. "They won't let me help them if they know who I am. Then they'll go up against Livio without the vital information I can provide, and it will be *your* fault."

"That's right." Euphy's voice and eyes hardened. "Someone else has to be at fault no matter what happens. You always have to be the hero, never in the wrong."

"Euphy," Dandy pleaded, his tone weakening in the face of Euphy's onslaught. "What about how we met? What about in the market? Wasn't I kind to you then?"

"That was because I was sufficiently in awe of you then. You don't like me so much now that I don't hang onto your every word, the way that lady does – the one whose servant you said you were. Livio's told me about her, and it's not hard to see why you'd pick someone like that; because she has no thoughts outside of what you tell her. You only like people you can dictate to. People you can control."

Euphy's voice was cold and stinging as metal in winter, and Dandy nearly staggered back from its blow. Ever since he'd met Theodora in the aftermath of the Night, he'd done his best to look out for her, even when it meant that his devotion to Livio had suffered. Even when it meant facing the anger of a unicorn, or trying to find someone who could.

He had thought his care was born of real affection, but to see things in these terms, to see their relationship stripped down to these harsh, bare bones, left him appalled. Was she really so dear to him because she had been so thoroughly conquered by him in the New Glory?

He could have told her the truth of what he was years ago. He could have tried to help her remember. But Euphy was right; he had chosen not to because it would've meant losing his place as her benefactor.

"Do what you want to her, but *I* won't be dictated to anymore. Not by you," Euphy continued with a tone no less able to be argued with than the unicorn's. "Now get out of here, Dandy, and don't you dare speak to me the way you do to her again, unless you want your little secret to get out in the camp."

Dandy could hardly recognize his own body obeying the command while the world felt like it was shaking under his feet. How could Euphy have seen into his true self like this, when Dandy himself hadn't even known it?

He had thought of himself as a fair and generous person – but was it true that he was really only kind because of what it would get him in the end? Adoration, admiration, a legion of "lessers" to look up to him, to prop him up with words of thanks and praise for having deigned to notice them?

Was that why he had decided to befriend Euphy in the first place, that day in the library? Or why he chose to join Castan's band – because he would be the insider who came from on high to offer them pearls of intelligence which no one else could provide?

In waves of revulsion, he saw that in each of these instances, and in so many others throughout his life of privilege and power, he *had* enjoyed the adulation his actions incited, much more than the pleasure that came from simply helping someone for its own sake. What he had enjoyed the most was being the one with all the answers, the one whose judgement was superior to everyone else's. The one being looked up to.

It was why he had kept the truth from Theodora. It was why he had joined Livio in the first place.

But the payment for that last one had come at last, and Dandy was stuck with Livio now. All hope of throwing off that yoke stood in danger of being obliterated at any moment, by one of the very people he had helped Livio conquer – someone who had apparently gained the rumored unicorn sight, for how else could he have cut so ruthlessly straight to Dandy's unknown heart?

With bowed head, he walked down the road toward the castle, where not one but two dreadful fires smoldered in the dungeon below – Euphemio and his unicorn – both creatures who could burn his courage to ashes, and he spent a night so restless that he couldn't fathom how he was going to face Livio in the morning and act as if he were the same person he'd been.

This was not the first time he'd regretted his part in the Night of New Glory, but he was discovering that admitting that something you'd done was wrong was quite different than admitting there was something wrong within yourself.

He wished he could go to Theodora. Even if he couldn't unburden his mind completely to her, being near her would at least be a calming influence. She would look at him gently, without condemnation, and though this was only because she didn't know she had a reason to, it would still feel better compared to Euphy's hard, accusing glare.

But he knew that mindlessly comforting words would be of no help. They would distract him, lull him into believing that he was good enough; they would never help him chart the depths of what was really in his heart, and certainly not to correct it. This was a journey he was going to have to make alone.

*   *   *

Euphy made it all the way back to the stable before any shade fell over his triumph. It had been vindicating to confront Dandy over his self-importance and half-truths, until Euphy remembered that he hadn't told Minari about his meeting with Livio, either.

He ought to tell. He *would* tell. Minari, wise as he was, would understand.

"Lots of things have happened in the past few days," he started, then decided that sharing the story of Dandy first would make it easier to justify the story of Livio later. "You remember how I told you about Dandy? I found out that he's actually supported Livio for years. Worked directly for him, even. He said he's changed his mind, but the thing that bothers me the most is how he –"

"I wouldn't trust anyone who consorts with *him*, whether they claim to have repented or not," huffed Minari, to which

Euphy outwardly agreed, though he couldn't finish the story after that.

The label of people who consorted with Livio – the type of people whom Minari couldn't trust – now included himself.

"*This is the start of it,*" he thought. The separation that was coming at the end of this revolution.

But if that was the way it had to be, then Euphy was going to prove that he was *not* what Dandy had said. He would get as close to Livio as he possibly could, then take what he learned there and deliver it to Vanya himself, knowing that each word would sever the ties that held him to Minari. He would pay the price of Minari's freedom with his own heart, and let no one dare say that Euphemio Benedetti had acted selfishly.

"I'll see you tomorrow, Minari," he said through the knot in his throat, trying not to think about how there were only so many more tomorrows those words could contain.

CHAPTER 16
Blood Tie

It was nearly three days since Dandy had seen his true self in the mirror of Euphy's eyes. Five days since he had seen Theodora.

It would have been wrong to see her now that he knew their relationship had been built on the fact that she was nothing but a prop to his ego. But after so long a time, he was beginning to ask himself whether it wouldn't be more wrong to continue to avoid her.

Whatever had been the reason for its beginning, the reality was that she did depend on him, and he couldn't stay away forever.

He was in the middle of lecturing himself that he shouldn't allow his vanity to be flattered by any joy she would show at his arrival when, to his surprise, he found her already out in the tapestried hall, on the arm of none other than Livio.

Dandy remembered what Livio had said not long ago about putting Theodora in her place, and nearly swayed on his feet as realized that if Euphy had met with Livio, he might have shared the facts of Dandy's changing allegiance. What if that was the reason Livio suddenly felt the need to show up here?

"Oh, Dandy, just the person I wanted to speak to," Livio said, unhooking his arm from Theodora's in one fluid motion.

"My lady, if you'll forgive me," he bowed to her with his hand over his heart. "I must speak to our friend here, and I'm afraid it would bore you terribly. Why don't you try that walk in the Upper Gardens we were talking of just now? I truly can't believe you haven't been there. The sunlight is quite beautiful in that part of the property, and it will do you good."

The Upper Gardens were Livio's private retreat, an open courtyard on the roof of the castle. Dandy had never taken Theodora there because it was not his place to do so. Livio and his closest circle were admitted to enter, but she did not have that right, at least not anymore. She'd probably been there many times when her father had still owned them.

"Take your dear lady to see my roses," Livio was saying to Marta, the maid, who twisting her hands in her apron as she trailed behind them. Next to her was Domenico, one of Livio's attendants, who looked more studiously dignified.

"My man will show you the way." Livio signalled for Domenico to lead the women away, and turned to Dandy.

"I'm disappointed in you," he said, smiling though the words did nothing to ease Dandy's fear. "You've never told me how charming a creature she is, though if I were in your position, I would want to keep her to myself, too."

Then, seeing how tensely Dandy stood, he broke into a laugh.

"Don't look so worried. I'm not angry at you. I never really troubled myself about needing her before anyway, so the timing comes out alright in the end."

Dandy exhaled, searching Livio's face.

Did he really not know what Dandy was doing behind his back? And if not, then why was he so interested in meeting Theodora?

"What do you mean by needing her? And by timing? The timing of what?"

"Oh, you know," Livio waved his hand. "All those people – Lord Kerlin and such – rattling on about me getting an heir. It always sounded like such a bother, but with all the reports of Ausonians getting restless these days, I think I can see the point now. It would calm the natives down if I had a blood tie to the throne."

"A blood tie…an heir?" Dandy choked on the words, feeling as if his stomach were dropping to the floor and rising in his throat the same time.

"You can't mean – "

"You don't think it's a good idea?" Livio asked quietly, his chin tilted down and his lip close to quivering.

Dandy tried to make himself lie, to say that it was a fine idea and avoid Livio's displeasure. But he couldn't force his mouth form the words.

"I think that is…a sound strategy," he finally got out. It was true; it *was* a good strategy for Livio. It just wasn't a good one for anyone else involved.

"I'm glad you think so," Livio straightened with pride. "I'll let you know how I get on. You'll advise me on the best way to go about things with her, won't you?"

Dandy barely managed something that might pass as a nod. There was no way he was going to be able to say what Livio wanted this time.

"Will there be anything else?" he asked instead. "I'm afraid I really must be going."

"I wish you could stay and tell me everything now," Livio sighed, "But if you have somewhere better to be, then we can talk about it later. I just wanted to tell you my news first, so that you wouldn't be caught off guard when it came out afterward. You've been keeping her so carefully, and I thought you'd want to know."

Livio had spoken truly there. Dandy *had* been careful in watching over Theodora, but he heard an edge in the words, as if Livio resented the fact that Dandy had had kept a treasure out of his hands.

But Dandy couldn't bear to stand and ponder that in front of Livio. He stiffly performed the customary bow before the king – still customary, even though they'd been friends these many years – and walked away with measured steps, though he could feel his blood pounding in what was nearing panic.

His first instinct was to run to the Upper Gardens, to explain the situation to Theodora, and to instruct her not to fall for Livio or his ideas. He was confident that she would do anything he told her.

But Euphy's words, piercing as steel, came back to him, "*You only like people you can dictate to*."

To warn Theodora off of Livio, to force her away from him, wouldn't that be imposing his own will on her? Who was he to say that she might not want to stay with Livio if she had the choice? She had been perfectly happy being under Dandy's direction, and Livio held his opinions even more strongly than Dandy did. What if that meant she'd be even happier with Livio than she'd been with him?

It was a terrible thought, but the choice was hers, and he must let her make it.

CHAPTER 17
Upper Gardens

Sunlight streamed through the windows of Prisma, leaving lancets of warmth on its stone floors. But Dandy was insensible to all of it. The halls which he couldn't now follow to Theodora's door felt cheerless even in midday.

If he spent too much time with her, Livio would be angry, and knowing him, it might drive Livio to shorten the timeline, to force Theodora into marriage sooner, rather than taking the time to try and win her over.

Livio preferred charm, but he took things by unforgiving force when he had to. He was not called the Iron Hand for nothing, and if he saw Dandy hovering around his key to a true claim on the throne, he would take any measures he saw necessary.

So Dandy could not go to Theodora's chambers as he was used to doing, but he remembered the Upper Gardens. If he came across her by chance there, Livio couldn't blame him for that.

The autumn wind was bracing when he stepped into the gardens, but the sun was out, and he found Theodora there as he'd expected. He had seen her in the sunlight before, but somehow, she seemed to glow more than she used to, even with the threat of Livio over her.

The bright rays which had brought Dandy no joy in the stone halls brought out brilliant shades of color in her hair which he rarely saw indoors, and her eyes looked like glass with the way they reflected every flower around her, and every wisp of cloud in the sky above.

His heart was suddenly banging in his chest, and the understanding crashed over him in that moment of why Livio's plan disgusted him so. It was more than just wanting what was a best for his ward.

"Of all the times to have such a revelation! Now that it's too late."

One week earlier, and he could have made his feelings known. But now, he couldn't even have the solace of knowing that she knew how he felt, nor of fantasizing that she might love him no matter what happened with Livio. Because if he allowed his own wishes to influence her decision, he would be doing just what Euphy had accused him of.

He had to remind himself of this many times in the following days as Livio enthusiastically shared the tales of his own pursuit, and Dandy had to pretend to hear them with equal enthusiasm.

It wouldn't have been easy prior to Dandy's ill-timed discovery. After it, Livio's tales were enough to test every ounce of the resolution Dandy had made.

"She's been with me to the Upper Gardens three times already," Livio was telling him as they stood together in the Emerald Room, where council meetings were usually held. "She's even started getting her maid to take her there without me. Already feeling free to do so, after so short a time!"

Dandy considered it a victory that he kept his eyes down, though he couldn't keep the sharpness entirely out of his voice when he asked, "Is she going because she wants to, or because you *told* her to?"

"Well, of course I've told her to go there. I can't be bothered to visit her every day. It's so much easier if she can just be where I am already. Besides, she'll think it's a chance meeting if I see her there, and people supposedly find chance meetings romantic, don't they?"

Dandy shivered at the mention of a chance meeting in the gardens, considering his own experience there, but Livio continued without noticing.

"So I can't go to her, and I very well can't bring her here." He gestured around at the room. "She'd be as lost as a rabbit."

"Is that so? Or do you just not want her here because she'd be in your way?" Dandy countered. He knew he was treading on dangerous ground, but he hoped to pass it off as simply wanting to counsel Livio. Ever since they'd known each other, it had been his job to help Livio plan the angles of any attack or strategic decision. Why should this particular decision to be any different?

But when Dandy said it, Livio's mouth turned downward, and he dropped his eyes to the floor in a look of injured sensitivity.

"I'm starting to suspect you think me unworthy of her. How could you view me so poorly after we've been friends all this time?"

"*All this time,* " Dandy reflected. Long ago, at the start, Livio had seemed so glamorous. The up-and-coming princeling who knew what he wanted and how to get it, who was so effortlessly charming in everything he did that even when he caused hurt to others, Dandy hadn't believed that he had in the least intended it.

That was why Dandy had followed him through blood and betrayal on the path toward the throne of Ausonia. Livio was a magnetizing force. He was the person everyone wanted to be, to follow, to serve. Though he and Livio were friends, it had felt natural back then for Livio to be the one to rule, and Dandy the one to help him do so.

But in this case, he found that he very much minded being second to Livio. He minded that Livio would exploit Theodora in such a mercenary manner.

But that was what Livio had always done –looked for vulnerabilities and exploited them – and Dandy had always known it. The very walls of this stolen castle attested to that, and the paintings in the Gallery of Battles bore witness to just how much Dandy had participated in Livio's brand of exploitation.

In fact, he had tried to do the very same thing to Euphy and his unicorn that Livio was now planning to do to Theodora – to get them to serve his own purposes, without considering whom it might hurt.

No wonder Euphy had been so upset at anyone trying to use the unicorn as a tool. Dandy knew now how awful it could be to have someone you cared for ripped away simply because they were useful to someone else's plans. And if he told the truth, Livio had responded to Dandy's concerns much more graciously than Dandy had to Euphy's.

Dandy had harangued Euphy for his supposed selfishness, but he was the one who had been self-important and arrogant, assuming that the whole world ought to bend to his own view.

Euphy could not know this, but it was what had made Dandy so effective as Livio's right hand in the coming of the New Glory. Dandy had not once stopped to question whether these Ausonians could want anyone other than Livio to lead them. For if Livio was glorious and necessary in Dandy's view, then that must be the objective truth. He must be glorious and necessary in the eyes of all.

It wasn't until he'd met Theodora that he'd realized anyone could see things from any other perspective, and even then, he still hadn't learned to afford that privilege to everyone. He certainly hadn't to Euphy.

He needed to apologize. That much was clear, and that much he could do. But Euphy would not let him get near. Anytime they were in the camp together, Euphy maneuvered to keep several people in between them, and when Dandy tried to urge the others to decide on a final course of action quickly, Euphy stood at the far end of the table, his accusing gaze flashing.

"How is rushing into things going to help us?" he asked.

Dandy hesitated. Though Theodora was Nereus's heir, and ought to be rightful ruler after Livio was deposed, he couldn't speak of her in front of everyone. It was too personal, and it might overwhelm her to have all these strangers suddenly looking to her as their savior. Though that was probably how Euphy had felt about the unicorn before Dandy had taken it upon himself to reveal its existence.

"I've heard…some things being said around the castle. Livio's making plans to solidify his claim to the throne, and not just through the unicorn."

"What else is he planning? What could be more effective than a unicorn?" asked Emmanuel.

"If you know what it is, do you know how we can prepare against it?" Vitalia added.

"Please do tell us," said Euphy, with a frosty smile. "I, for one, would like to know exactly where, or *whom*, you heard this from."

Dandy stammered, and he regretted that his behavior in his rush to help Theodora the first time had cost him any help he might have looked for now that a greater danger was facing her.

"It was just some gossip I'd heard," he said, knowing that he sounded exactly as small as Euphy wanted him to. "Something about how he wants an Ausonian heir. But he hasn't even got a woman yet."

With luck, he never would.

"*If* that's true," said Euphy. "We'd be better off investigating first. If we launched a whole attack to save some hypothetical woman, what would we do if we got there and found out she didn't exist? We'd be in too deep for no reason, and if any of us did escape, it would make us shy to act when the right moment did come."

"You haven't heard anything about this in the castle yourself?" Emmanuel asked, looking at Euphy.

Euphy was gratified that it was *him*, and not Dandy, that Emmanuel turned to for information, and that Dandy had been brought so low that he didn't dare speak against Euphy now.

Yes, knowing Livio made things much easier.

CHAPTER 18
Janus

Dandy couldn't say that he felt any better about Livio's plan for Theodora, but being forced to constantly hear about it at least allowed him to get over the initial shock. He could think straight enough now to try and formulate an argument against it which Livio might listen to. He couldn't give every one of his real reasons, but what he *could* say was more logical, in any case.

"Let's look at things clearly," he said. "If you pick Theodora because of her ties to the throne, people will say it's because you know you had no real right to it in the first place. They're restless enough already; if you have a child with her…" Dandy forced himself to talk past the wave of nausea that rolled through him.

"It won't appease them, but it *will* give them something to rally around. A new heir to the house of Nereus – one they might think they can depose you in favor of."

"I'd like to see them try," Livio predictably retorted.

"But you *are* worried it could happen. That's why you've gotten the unicorn, isn't it? And why you've thought of Theodora in the first place?

Please think about it. After we worked so hard to get rid of that family, what good would it do to add a new prince or princess to their line? If you have to pick an Ausonian woman, let it be someone who's not of noble blood. That way, the child's only claim to the throne would be through you."

"How many women do you know, Dandy? Ausonian ones, I mean…besides our friend Theodora?"

Dandy didn't respond. There were many Ausonian women in Castan's camp, but as with everything else these days, he couldn't mention them, and he knew for a fact that they'd have zero interest in being Livio's bride, anyway.

"It's alright, I understand," said Livio, his voice suddenly as delicate as if he were speaking to a hurt animal.

Was he agreeing to the request so soon? Could it really be so uncomplicated?

"She's been yours for a long time," he explained. "Of course you'd be jealous. But you could have her back again afterward. I suppose I wouldn't really need her beyond a certain point. I could live without her if it meant that much to you." Livio offered, looking so like a martyr that Dandy could almost believe that he really was making some beneficent sacrifice – until the implication of his words sank in.

Dandy wouldn't have thought it possible for blood to drain from his face and rush into his cheeks at the same time, but he felt himself managing this feat as he struggled to find a way to respond.

Even though things weren't like that with Theodora, Dandy was used to Livio implying the opposite. But it was the first time he'd suggested something like *this*, that they could share in…whatever Livio thought they were doing. It would have been hard enough to hear before that sunny day in the Upper Gardens, and it was doubly painful now. But the worst part was that Livio saw nothing wrong with the arrangement he was proposing.

"It would be nice to be able to enjoy something for myself, especially after you've already had plenty of opportunity, but that's what a king does – sacrifices for the people who depend on him." He twisted the jeweled ring on his right hand morosely.

"Have you informed her of your intentions in all this?" Dandy asked slowly.

"A gentleman doesn't speak of such things bluntly. It would be improper to mention marriage, or anything else, until I was absolutely assured of her affections."

Dandy pushed down the flutter of hope in his heart at that the knowledge that Livio was not yet "absolutely assured."

"Then you haven't spoken to her about an heir? She doesn't know that giving you her affection will lead her to that?"

Livio shook his head.

"But she has to be told. I don't imagine she knows you'd expect this of her."

"Do we tell our stud horses, or our brood mares, when they're going to be used to bring us something useful? You must admit she probably wouldn't be able to understand it any more than they would be, even if I were coarse enough to mention it to her."

"Any more than an *animal?*"

"Haven't we always said that's what Ausonia is good for? To use for its resources?" Livio asked, looking surprised. "Why would that be wrong now? If it's because you were there first, I said you could have her back after it's done, didn't I? Though…" he trailed off, musing. "I'd have to exercise my privilege as a husband again if something should happen to the first child. Even you would have to see the logic in that."

"*Heaven help us,*" thought Dandy. He did not want to get into a contest with Livio over who had more of a claim on Theodora's body.

"Well," Livio said aggrievedly when Dandy didn't answer. "You can go, if all this is so bothersome to you. And don't worry, I won't tell you any more of the details. I'll just muddle my way through on my own, since you'd rather not help me."

So Dandy got his wish, though he found that not hearing Livio's news came with its own set of worries, for he no longer had any way of knowing just how close Theodora was to her fate.

In the days after that horrible conversation, he noticed the way some of the other nobles gave him surreptitious glances as he passed. He was sure the king had been telling them of how cruel and selfish Dandy was to keep him from the supposed love of his life. He wished he were as clever at doing so in reality as he was in Livio's fiction.

He didn't much care if he were being maligned, but he did fear what it might mean for Theodora. If Livio were jealous enough of their relationship, Dandy knew him well enough to know that he might dispense with all his high talk of polite courtship and take her by force and violence, the same way he had taken her country.

At this point, Dandy thought his best chance was pleading the case before the morrismen. He would tell them the truth of everything, and even if they hated him for it, it would be worth it if he could convince them to turn the missing princess of Ausonia into their rallying point now, rather than later.

He was on the brink of going to them, though it was still morning, when he received a summons telling him that Livio wished to see him in the Emerald Room, for the first time in days.

He was sure that this would be to hear the official announcement of Livio's betrothal, and he slid glumly into his seat around the council table. All of the other members were already there, and Dandy realized how much he must have been dragging his feet to be this late.

Livio stood and took a breath, while Dandy held his.

"Friends, wicked forces are on the move in our land. As many of you know, a seditious rebel from among the people has been captured in the market, and sentenced to death by hanging tomorrow afternoon."

136

Dandy looked around the room. He barely even had time to register relief that this wasn't about Theodora. He had heard nothing about a traitor or a hanging, and his chest tightened as he thought of the morrismen near the market. Who among them had been taken?

"But this has not been enough. Evil has been working not only on the outside, but within our own walls." Livio was shifting into a grandiose tone, which Dandy recognized as the one he saved for speeches meant to rouse people to action. "Someone who was once one of our own has been creeping among us like a wolf among sheep, sowing discord and speaking treason.

As we captured the rebel through quick and decisive measures, this threat also requires swift action by those of us who still uphold virtue. This wicked man has made us believe that he had the best interests of the kingdom at heart."

By this time, Dandy's heart was banging in his chest. Not as it did when he'd looked at Theodora in the sunlight amongst the flowers, but as a warning bell ringing out that Livio had finally discovered his connection to the morris dancers.

"He has been harassing the former princess of Ausonia, whom I have allowed to stay under my roof and my protection out of nothing but compassion, and whom I have left alone out of the purest respect.

Yet he has been stalking her every day, filling her head with lies about me, trying to prevent my suit of her, and thereby prevent the more peaceful union of Albion and Ausonia. If he succeeds with her, how many others may he poison with his lies? How much strife and even bloodshed, like that of the poor misguided rebel, will be caused by such malevolence?"

Somehow, through the billows of emotion for Theodora, the morrismen, and himself, it dawned on Dandy that Livio hadn't mentioned him in relation to the real rebellion at all. All of his complaints so far were limited to the issue of

137

Theodora, and even those were not accurate to the truth. In fact, they were the complete opposite of everything Dandy had really been doing.

"As the caretaker of all of my people, it is my responsibility to put a stop to anyone who works against the cause of right." Livio's voice was rising to an intense pitch. "Yet it is from you, my people, that I gain the strength to do this. Will you lend me your support? Will you stand together with me against evil?"

He raised his arms before him as if to elevate the spirits of his listeners, and not a one save Dandy hesitated to stand as he did so.

How effective Livio's words were, and how Dandy knew they would be. They were the same words an ambitious noble had used to convince a young military man to rob a king of his throne, a prince of his future, and a princess of her memories.

But they would not convince this soldier a second time.

He did stand then, not waiting for any of them to gain enough honor to look at him directly, and swept out the door, his boot heels echoing in the marble room.

He briefly wondered whether Livio would order the others to stop him, but even if they tried, he wasn't called the Morningstar for nothing, and everyone else there knew it.

No, Livio's plan had been to force Dandy to leave of his own volition. He'd assumed that being accused of disloyalty to Livio was the worst thing that could happen to him, and that being shamed and singled out for this would be too much for Dandy to bear.

Livio was getting what he wanted – Dandy knew he couldn't stay here any longer – but it wasn't because he was shamed by anything Livio had said. Did Livio even know what forcing him out was actually enabling him to do?

Dandy could now throw all of his power into reclaiming the throne, without worrying whether it would give him away to Livio. He no longer had to sit passively and feign agreement with Livio's self-serving speeches, no longer had to balance his real feelings with the behavior expected of him. All obligation to do that was gone, removed by Livio himself.

If he had suspected what Dandy was really doing, he wouldn't have needed to cook up those accusations of "harassing the princess." He could easily have stood Dandy up on the gallows with the rebel he'd captured. But he'd had to invent an excuse to run Dandy out, which was a good sign.

And it was just in time. If Livio had waited to accuse Dandy until after the hanging of this unknown morrisman, then Dandy, being still in Livio's service, would have been expected to participate in rejoicing over it. But he could fly to the camp now without compunction, to save whichever of them was facing the noose.

His mind ran relentlessly over who it might be, sorting through the many faces who belonged to the camp. What if it were Euphy, and Dandy had driven him right into Livio's grasp with his rough words?

If Euphy became another innocent person to die because of Dandy, in spite of how hard he'd been trying to correct his mistakes, would any of his efforts ever mean anything?

He'd even refused to dictate to Theodora how she should feel toward Livio when he would have dearly loved to, and he'd had the power to do it right there in his hand, but Euphy might never know it.

Theodora…so there was one thing keeping him from leaving this castle without looking back. He had to see her first.

If Livio had planned this public denunciation on one front, and a public hanging on another, it wasn't out of the question that he really would move to take Theodora by force at the same time.

He knew that Livio was trying to draw the rebels out, and he would have given almost anything to go to them, to tell them to find some other way to save their lost one, but he couldn't leave Theodora defenseless. If he tried to flee with her to the morris camp, it would hardly be safer than here, yet he couldn't bring himself to take her somewhere far away from everything else that he bore responsibility for.

Striking on all fronts, all at once had been his and Livio's favored tactic in the past. Ambushing and exhausting the enemy's resources with simultaneous offensives was how they had gained Ausonia the first time. And if Dandy had thought he'd understood how the Ausonians felt back then, he understood it more than ever now – what it felt like to know that Livio was moving on him, and to not know which way he should take to escape.

CHAPTER 19
I'm Not Afraid

"I'm telling you, there's got to be a better way. If we could just – "

Bridle stopped when he saw his listeners smirking in the firelight.

"There he goes again," said Fiora, who had once been a hired hand alongside him his shepherding days. She rolled her eyes for the benefit of those who sat beside her.

"Again? When have I told you about this before?" Fiora wasn't part of the Command Rooms, and their usual conversations around the evening fires didn't normally include discussions of what went on in them. Bridle had only brought up it up tonight out of desperation, and even then, he hadn't shared the details.

"Castan says you're always going on about you know better than he does."

Bridle had assumed that she'd be a friendly ear, considering their shared background.

But when he told her as much, she replied "I *have* known you a long time, haven't I? Do you remember that time when you were learning about dragons, and how hard you tried to convince us to build little suits of armor for the sheep, so a dragon couldn't come and eat them? Or when you got so busy trying to watch for dragons in the sky that you walked right into a ditch?"

Bridle recalled exactly the incidents to which she was referring. He also remembered that he was no more than twelve years old at the time.

"So you're going to judge my worth now based on some mistakes I made half my life ago?"

Was everyone in this camp going to worship at the altar of the past forever?

"If that's how everyone feels, then what are we even doing here? If who we were in the past is all we'll ever be, what's the point of any of this? Why are we claiming to want to change the future if nobody thinks it's even possible?"

It was becoming evident to Bridle that if he wanted to improve the future or even the present, this camp was not the place for him. Here, he would forever be seen as misinformed child to be talked down to and laughed at behind their hands, or else scolded and punished for questioning a consensus that was ill-planned and unwise.

He wouldn't have even minded if the things he were getting shouted at for were actual breaches of conduct. He himself had given a lecture or two to members of his own squadron who had gotten out of line. But his own biggest sin seemed to be using the perfectly sound mind that he'd been given to actually look at the reality of the situation.

And he was going to use that sound mind to find some other way to do his part against Livio. Maybe he'd go to the castle; try to pick up work there. He'd organize another rebel faction starting with himself, Euphy, and Dandy. Three was enough to get something moving.

As a matter of fact, if Castan had ever actually listened to Bridle instead of assuming he was an ignorant good-for-nothing, he might have found that they'd had more in common than he thought. Bridle remembered what Castan had said to Golden on the first night Euphy had come to them.

"*You knew him **when** he was a child. Not **since**. Things change in that amount of time. People change.*"

It was the same thing Bridle had tried to say to Fiora. In another life, Castan might have been a useful ally in this new plan. But that other life would require Castan to apply his principles to himself and his own views, and the chances of that happening were non-existent. In Castan's mind, Golden couldn't be questioned in spite of no longer being what he had once been, but Euphy couldn't be trusted for the very same reason – *because* he was no longer what he once had been. It was illogical, and yet Bridle was the one accused of being foolish.

Well, Castan would soon be free of the burden of Bridle's ideas. In the morning, Bridle would go to him and give his notice. He wanted to do it tonight, but he didn't want to deal with getting into a fight about it this late in the evening. Besides, looking for a new place to sleep in the cold of a winter night wasn't an inviting prospect.

He would do it after morning muster, where he count the troops off one last time – a good shepherd making sure all of his sheep were accounted for before selling them at market.

Every year when he'd done that with his flocks, he'd wanted his sheep to go somewhere where they'd be well taken care of, but in the end, it wasn't up to him. The owners of the animals – people far richer than Bridle – were the ones who got to decide that, and the flocks usually went to whomever paid the most, not who promised to treat them the best. He'd be leaving his charges in Castan's hands, and he was no more powerful to help them than he had been with the sheep.

When morning came, he walked down the rows with Emmanuel and Vitalia, counting the dancers who shivered in the morning air, but when they went to report the numbers at the head of the assembly, only Golden was there, attended by Tobiah. Castan was not with them

143

"He's at the market," Tobiah explained. "Astor and Paulina didn't get enough flour for breakfast when they went to the market yesterday, so he went to do it himself."

"And he had to go in the middle of muster?" Bridle groused at him.

Two new recruits miscalculating on their first supply run hardly sounded like a reason to break routine, but leave it to Castan to get so worked up over something so pointless.

"*You* going to tell all of these people there's nothing to eat this morning?"

"What I'm going to do is go look for him. It'll be better than just sitting around here waiting for him to come back."

"Since when are you so anxious to be in his presence?"

"I've got something important to talk to him about," said Bridle evasively.

As he crossed the frost-dusted field to the market, he remembered the days of minding sheep with no shelter from the cold. Being with this group had gotten him out of *that*, but there was so much more he could be beyond just a suffering shepherd or a suffering morris dancer, and he was going to find it.

But he had to find Castan first, and that was proving difficult, for neither the flour vendor, nor any of the others Bridle asked, had seen him.

"I swear if he changed his mind and went back to camp while I was out here freezing for him," Bridle said to himself, though the countless analyses of spaces, shapes, numbers, and time which had run in the back of his mind for as long as he could remember plainly showed him that they would have had to cross each other along the path unless Castan had for some reason taken a needlessly long and convoluted stroll along the perimeter of the meadow before returning home.

Knowing this, he next tried the guards at the peace officers' station where he'd once helped deposit the young livestock rustler. But when he described Castan to them,

144

they looked at him sideways and told him he'd be better off not asking any questions about that.

"Sir," protested Bridle, indignation flaring up in him at once again being treated like a bothersome child. "I wouldn't come to you if it weren't something important. I helped chase a thief all the way across this market some weeks ago, and you weren't too busy to listen to me then."

Remembering how he, Euphy, and Dandy had worked so well together made Bridle optimistic for what the three of them could accomplish away from the endless dithering and disrespect of the Command Room, and he half forgot the guard he'd been speaking to a moment ago, until that guard said,

"All the more reason for you to leave this matter alone, son. It's no business of law-abiding folk."

"What do you mean, 'no business?' What's happened?" Bridle asked, a sudden suspicion pulling him down from his rosy visions of the future.

"Didn't I just tell you to leave it alone?" was all the man would say.

Bridle looked around the market, swallowing the protest on his tongue and the unease that slid down with it. The most obvious thing was also the worst one. If Castan had been discovered as rebel, they were all in danger, and Bridle might implicate himself by caring too much. But he had to know how much trouble they were in.

He couldn't ask any more around the market, lest the officers see him doing it, or whoever it was that had turned Castan in notice him as well. So in the end, he decided on asking at the houses along the side of Clockface that led to the town proper, to find out if anyone might have seen something out of their windows, away from the listening ears of the peace officers.

"I'm looking for a friend of mine. Someone said he came this way," Bridle repeated the words he'd already spoken many times that morning, describing Castan to a woman who was holding a broom in her doorway.

"I did see someone like that," said the woman, adjusting the scarf tied around her hair. "Being dragged up the road by those royal muscle guards. They were on the stretch for sure, having to haul a great big man like that. And him fighting them all the way."

"Dragged? By royal men? All the way to where?" Bridle felt the words bubbling up almost faster than he could say them.

"To the castle, I'd say. When any of them were able to catch their breath, I heard a bit about him getting the traitors' reward. It wouldn't be the first time. You see a lot of that when you live here."

She said it without any particular emotion, but Bridle's knees buckled at the thought. It made no sense, he knew, for prior to this moment, he'd been fervently wishing to never see Castan again. He ought to be rejoicing, but all he could do was slump against the doorframe, nailed there by the woman's impassive words. It seemed his wish was going to come horribly true.

The woman had gone to the well in her small yard and back before Bridle found the strength to lift his forehead from where it had dropped against the weathered boards.

"Did you hear anything else?" he managed to ask after a shaky sip from the ladle she'd handed him, which sent splashes down onto his collar. "How much do you know about what they do to traitors?"

He already knew the answer, of course, but he pleaded silently that this woman might give him some answer, any answer, that could let him believe otherwise.

She did not.

She explained to him that nobody she'd known who'd been accused of treason had ever come back home from the castle.

"Don't tell anyone that you've told me this." He could hear his voice trembling.

"Sure, if you don't want me to," she answered. "But I'm not afraid of them."

There was no show of bravado as she said it. In fact, she barely even looked up from the sweeping she'd already resumed. She spoke it as simply as everything else she'd said so far, as if it were all a just a matter of fact, and Bridle, in spite of his mounting despair, reflected that she would have been a good recruit for the rebellion. Better than *him*, for he was fighting to stand on his own feet while she'd already gone back to her housework.

But there was no time for gloomy comparisons now. There was no time for anything but to go back to camp and beg Golden to give the word to save Castan.

All these weeks they'd spent discussing what to do, and look where it had gotten them. Livio could hurt them just as much as ever. It was what Bridle had been warning against for so long. What Castan had insisted he was being too hasty about. If Castan had listened to him, he could have saved himself from facing the gallows. Yet that stupid stubbornness had led him to his own demise.

Bridle slammed his hand against the doorframe's splintery wood, and got a stinging jolt from his fingertips to his wrist in return. The shock of it wrung tears from his eyes, though he was aware that they might have spilled out even without it.

"Are you alright?" the woman asked, but he forced himself upright, knowing that if he didn't, he'd be collapsing on the ground next, and then he might never get up.

"I'm fine," he lied, stumbling out into the suddenly incongruous sunlight. "Thank you."

"Hope you get him back," she called.

His breath was ragged by the time he charged into Golden's tent, and it wasn't long before the other two

147

captains were called in after him. Orders were given through the camp that no one was to set foot outside of it save for Serena, the most fleet-footed member, who was dispatched to discreetly gather what intelligence she could from the market.

When she returned, she bore in her hand an official-looking paper with scrolled letters inked across it.

Golden took it, and Bridle tried not crowd him as he leaned in to look at the words on the page.

ANNOUNCEMENT:

Sanctioned by His Majesty, King Livio, with the authority of his own divine right and the consecration conferred on him by a blessed unicorn of Ausonia, be it known that a hanging of the traitor Castan Lorusso will occur in the plaza of Clockface Market at noon on this fourth day of the tenth month, in the twentieth year of New Glory.

Which traitor's guilt was revealed by said unicorn's sight, and whose punishment was determined by His Majesty's own most excellent judgement.

Let all citizens who cherish peace and security join the Peace Force in rejoicing over the wisdom,

prudence, and skill of our king, and his dedication to eliminating every threat to the safety and unity of our country.

Pietro Roseborough,
Chief Peace Officer of Clockface,
Peace Force of Ausonia General

"All who cherish peace and security," Vitalia clicked her tongue. "In other words, everyone who doesn't want to be next ought to keep quiet if they disapprove."

Bridle was ready to rush to Castan's rescue at that very moment, but Golden laid a hand on his arm.

"That's what Livio wants," he said. "To draw us out, to see whether we're really here, what our numbers look like. If he can get us to show ourselves now, and defeat us, he won't have to worry about what we might do him later."

Bridle was puzzled that he hadn't seen the truth of Golden's words before. It was a strategy that was clear as day now that he considered it. But the ever-running calculations in his mind had been obscured by the vortex of panic that was building inside of him. He shuddered to think what he might have done if Golden hadn't been there to cut through it.

"*Funny*," thought Bridle. He had always been the one to suggest that Golden be replaced as their leader, for pure practicality's sake, while Castan had been the one who argued for Golden's worth. Now Bridle was the one for whom practicality was no longer a fair trade for the value of one man. Perhaps he was more like Castan than he'd realized. He wouldn't mind that at all.

But any comfort in this idea was frozen over by the remembrance that whatever he had absorbed of Castan's personality might be the only trace left of that man after tomorrow.

To the others, Golden and Bridle looked as if they had switched personalities – Golden now speaking in decisive tones while Bridle's usually-vibrant face was vacant save for the shimmer of tears in his unfocused eyes.

To be forbidden from trying to save Castan. To run the risk of not seeing him alive again…As hard as that would be for Bridle, what would Castan think if he looked at the crowd from the scaffold, and Bridle wasn't there?

He would understandably think that Bridle held such a grudge that he wouldn't care enough to be there in Castan's last moments. He wouldn't know how much Bridle was regretting every hard word he'd said in every fight they'd had.

He could see now that they'd both been sincere in wishing for the plan to succeed, but he rued how such sincerity had caused such passionate disagreements, and that it would no doubt now lead Castan to dig his heels into his own doom. For when the old goat was questioned about the identity of the other rebels, Bridle knew he would refuse to speak. But if he would crack a little, he might be spared.

"*Give them my name, at least.*" Bridle thought. "*I don't mind taking it to help you.*"

But everyone there knew that the more the enemy tried to force Castan to speak, the less likely he was to comply. Many of them praised him for this, though Bridle saw that it was probably another reason why Livio had decided on the hanging so soon: as punishment for his belligerent refusal. He wouldn't put it past Castan to have spit in Livio's face.

"*But...!*" It was the first sparkle of possibility that had appeared to him all day. There were others in the castle who might appease Livio, who might be able to mitigate some of the damage Castan had done to himself.

"What about Dandy? He knows lots of courtiers. Could he convince them to tell Livio to delay it? Or can we ask Euphy? If nothing else, he could tell us a little of what's going on inside."

"I wouldn't count on their being able to come to us with all of this going on," Golden said. "It was a good thought, though. You're using that head of yours."

"Lucky us," Bridle said. "The people who would be most useful are kept away just when we need them most."

Emmanuel looked at him squarely. "What else is to be expected when what makes them valuable in the first place is the fact that they live within the enemy's walls?"

He'd spoken the truth, and his words had given Bridle a worse thought. What if the two from the castle weren't coming because they didn't *want* to? What if they had been the ones to turn Castan over to Livio? Bridle asked Golden about it, but the prince shook his head.

"If they had wanted to betray us, they could have told Livio our names themselves. They wouldn't have needed to go through Castan for that."

"But if they're on our side, then I hate to not use every option we've got," said Bridle. "Two whole friends there, maybe not five hundred steps from wherever Castan is right now, and we're just not going to *do* anything with that?"

"What do you propose?" Emmanuel asked. "Launching an assault on the stone palace itself, to get them out of there? If we can't storm the gibbet with any amount of confidence, do you think we could storm Prisma under these same circumstances?"

"Livio did it back then, during the New Glory. And isn't that what we've been planning to do all along? When will we ever do it, if not now?"

"Livio was not being looked for, or being drawn out with bait. We were planning to do it like he did – unannounced. Not like this. Besides, if he's really gotten the unicorn's power, that makes things all the more difficult for us."

Golden saw Bridle's shoulders go tense, then sag. This whipping back and forth between emotions would not help him, or any of them. This Golden knew from experience, so he spoke to keep Bridle focused on anything other than what was going on inside of his head.

"We'll wait for them until tomorrow morning. Euphy first came to us by night, do you remember? He may come that way again. If neither of them appear by that time, we'll move ahead without them."

For the first time that Bridle could remember, looking at the plain facts failed to bring him any joy. Castan was chained up just like that poor unicorn, Euphy and Dandy were inaccessible, and Bridle couldn't do a thing about any of it.

With so many threads unravelling at the same time, the idea of a bold and quick offensive which he'd always leaned on as the soundest of principles was falling apart beneath him, and none of the strategies writing themselves in his mind were able to stitch it back together in satisfactory way.

But the conflict was coming for them all now, whether they could piece themselves together or not.

CHAPTER 20
Red Moon

The light through the windows in the Rainbow Hall looked less like the gentle pools of before, and more like confused torrents bursting and spilling over Euphy. He squinted against their brilliance, and could just see through his eyelashes, Livio sprawled over his throne, staring at the ceiling with his legs draped over the armrest, looking deep in thought.

And he had good reason to be, Euphy thought. The news was everywhere, reaching even down to the stable. Castan had been arrested and was to receive a spectacle of an execution.

That was why Euphy had come. He meant to try and convince Livio that it wasn't worth it to go to all this trouble.

Dario had, for once in Euphy's whole memory of him, left the stable in the middle of the day, going down to Clockface for information on the injustice to his countryman, so Euphy was free to make his way to the castle's upper stories. He had no need of Stregatto's escort this time, as Livio had given Euphy a standing invitation to come any time he liked. And that, if for no other reason, made him glad that he'd gotten to know the king, for he was in a position now to help Castan in a way that he couldn't have done if he'd stayed a good little stableboy and never attempted to rise above his station.

After a moment, Livio's eyes left the vaulted ceiling and brightened when he saw Euphy, though he didn't rise from his slumped position in the chair.

"Euphy! I'm so glad that you've come, with all of… " he put a hand on his forehead and waved the other wearily in the air. "…With all of *this* going on. It's been such a day, and I could use a friendly ear."

"All of this? You mean the prisoner? You make it sound like you didn't intend for it to happen." If that were true, maybe Livio wouldn't need much convincing at all.

"Of course I didn't. I don't harm on anyone in my kingdom."

"Then why not let him go?"

"Because that would only bring more harm to others. It's such a difficult position to be in, you know, to have to weigh these things. I could almost wish I weren't the one it fell to."

"You don't *have* to do it," Euphy said, a little eagerly, and pulled himself back. "I mean, not right away. You don't have to decide his guilt right now.

And have you confirmed that he's really done anything in the first place? It won't make anybody in the town very happy to know that one of their own was punished for something he didn't do."

"He's not even one of their own," Livio pouted. "From what I gather, he's newly arrived in town, and he's been accusing me of such awful things."

Euphy couldn't imagine where Livio would have heard this, as Castan and all the morrismen were particular about not sharing any views in public which would give them away. Though he forbore to ask about that, and pressed on, "Whether he is or not, I imagine that such a hard sentence, so soon, will make other people think he was right."

"Don't you see?" Livio's voice grew thin, as if he were holding back tears. "I *have* to do it this way. If I don't, others will think they can try the same things. They'll be encouraged to hurt me and all of us in this castle. If I could have found another way, I would gladly have dispensed with all of this. And I've tried and tried to make myself stronger to keep this type of thing from happening, but…" his voice broke then, and there were definitely tears welling up in his eyes.

"I just can't figure out what I'm supposed to do to get the unicorn to help me."

He turned his glittering gaze to Euphy. "Isn't there anything you know of that would earn his help? I meant to ask you before, but I didn't want you to think I was using you just for that."

"Weren't you?" Euphy asked, startled by his own bluntness. It was true that Livio hadn't yet pressed him for information about Minari, but Euphy hadn't forgotten that the unicorn was the reason he had been summoned to the Rainbow Hall in the first place.

Livio gasped. "I did want to meet you because of that at first. But after we became friends, and you were so nice, it felt wrong to try to ask you for it. Now that Dandy has turned on me, you're the only friend I have left, and I don't want to lose you."

"Dandy has…?" Euphy asked, his breath catching. No reports regarding *him* had reached the stable. And while he didn't care whether Dandy went to the devil, the fact that his name was being mentioned at the same time as Castan's capture made him uneasy. How much had Livio actually found out? Did he know of the link between the two of them?

"What happened with Dandy?" he asked, trying not to be too obvious with how he dried his sweating palms on his sleeve cuffs.

"Oh," said Livio in a tormented tone. "He somehow decided that I wasn't good enough to be in his presence anymore. Being a dreadful nag wasn't anything new for him, but recently, it was as if I couldn't turn around without him there berating me, telling me that everything I wanted was wrong."

Livio's looked down, his chin quivering. Euphy could see the red glimmer of tears caught in the windows' light as they fell to the floor, and felt his heart twist in unexpected sympathy.

He well knew how it felt to be broken on the wheel of Dandy's rebuke, and he could easily believe that even a king could be reduced to tears by the spike of the Morningstar's tongue.

Even if Livio had deserved it (*"And he **had** deserved it, hadn't he?"*), Euphy's heart burned at this further proof of Dandy's insufferable self-righteousness. If he had given Livio the same kind of dressing down as he had given to Euphy, it would have been because that was what Dandy did with everyone. It was no credit to him having reproached someone who deserved it, when he did the same thing to others who did not.

"That man just doesn't stop," Euphy muttered, more to himself than anything, but Livio heard it, and looked at him with gratitude shining through his wounded expression.

"I knew you'd understand."

"What was he onto you for this time?"

"Oh," said Livio, and his face turned pinker in the window light. "I – I'm thinking of getting married, and he didn't believe I'd made a good choice for the match. But it's for the benefit of our country, you know. Even though I've tried my best, there are some of people – that prisoner, for example – who don't like how I do things. So I thought if I could marry an Ausonian lady, it might help them feel better. I hate to see any of our people unhappy, and if I can show that we're all united as one through this marriage, it would so relieve my mind.

If Dandy hadn't discouraged me from pursuing her, we might have been married already, and that poor prisoner might have been at peace. If he'd had the chance to see a

156

world like that, maybe he wouldn't have felt so driven to do what he's done. And I wouldn't need to pronounce this awful judgment on him."

"Then do you really need to do it? Why not give him time to change his mind first? He might be so grateful to you that he'd preach your virtues for the rest of his days."

Euphy knew that Castan was not likely to do this in the least, but he didn't have to tell Livio that.

"Listen to my friend speaking like a scholar," Livio noted, looking proud before his face fell again. "This is for the good of everyone, though. If he were allowed to go free, he would drag others into his sad delusions, and more people would end up hurting themselves, like he has. I can't take the chance of him causing that. I've heard there are already others like him. "

"What others?" Euphy pressed. Who else was at risk of sharing Castan's fate?

"I wish I knew. But you, Euphy – you might help me there."

Euphy went stiff for a moment, until he saw that Livio was smiling.

"You're Ausonian, aren't you? Have *you* heard anything? Do you know of anyone who's been spreading ideas like that?"

"I haven't heard anything about it," Euphy lied.

"What a pity. If you had, we could get to them before their minds were twisted. I was hoping the unicorn could help me save anyone like that. Wouldn't he have the ability to identify people who were in peril of succumbing to something so dreadful?

I haven't been clever enough to know how to ask him, though. If I knew, we could be done with all of this, and he could go back home. I hate to think of how he must be suffering, but I can't let him go until I've saved my people from this...*plague* of poisoned thinking. I wouldn't sacrifice their well-being even for that of a unicorn."

This was just how Euphy had felt when he'd weighed the morrismen's needs against Minari's. He'd felt that he could not sacrifice the unicorn's well-being even for the rebels', but it was a terrible choice to consider, and it occurred to Euphy that Livio might be suffering just as much under the same burden.

Had it been wrong for Livio to take Minari? Of course. But what if Livio hadn't *known* that Minari was capable of feeling all the things he was? Euphy himself hadn't known anything about it at the start; what if Livio had thought Minari was merely another dumb animal like the rest of the horses? Nobody objected to keeping a horse locked up in the stable, to be used when you needed it. And Euphy himself had broken many wild horses to accept a bit and saddle – how could he blame Livio for attempting to do the same in his ignorance?

What if…? What if Euphy were to help Livio understand what Minari was really like? What if he could help Livio see that Minari wasn't just some tool to be used?

"*He's scared to death of the beast. He knows it would kill him if he got too close,*" Stregatto had once said. But if Euphy could convince Minari to let Livio near for the sake of his own freedom, wouldn't that solve every-one's dilemma?

If Livio really believed that Minari could discern who was a threat and who wasn't, what if Minari told Livio to let Castan go? Then Livio could see that there was no need to hurt either of them, and they could both be freed.

But – and Euphy couldn't believe he was asking himself this – who was going to tell the morrismen that there was no need to hurt Livio?

For the very first time, amongst all the worry for everyone else involved in this storm that had swept all of them up, Euphy felt that Livio might be a victim in it, too.

It was true that he had come to Ausonia through violence, but Euphy wasn't certain that this man who blushed and sighed and shed tears over the hurt that had been done to him, would choose the same course of action now, or that he would not be moved by Minari's plight once he understood it. Vanya had changed in the years which had passed since Livio's arrival. Livio himself might have done the same.

Euphy was the only one who knew the full story of every party involved in these events. What if it was his destiny to tie them all together, to make them see each other as they really were, and to bring the game to its conclusion without any of them getting hurt? What if this was how he, the poor man with the lofty name, fulfilled his potential to become quality?

When Vanya became king again, wouldn't it secure Euphy the respect and attention to be remembered by him and his new court? Wouldn't it make him worthy to stay by Minari's side?

Euphy took a breath, the air in his lungs pressing against the heart full of new revelations. "Would you be willing to meet the unicorn? If he could tell you that there was nothing to worry about, would it help? If he told you that you could let the prisoner go, would you do it?"

"Does he speak to you?" Livio's full attention had snapped to him,

"Ah, not exactly," Euphy lied again. There were some details about Minari that shouldn't be shared even now.

"But I'm probably just not important enough for it. He might speak to you, since you're a king."

"Would he really be willing to speak to me? I know I could believe anything he told me if I could just hear it in his own voice."

This was how Euphy found himself racing to the dungeon, to plead with Minari to put his instincts aside just long enough to convince Livio to let him go free.

"Minari, please don't ask me questions about it now," he pleaded, "but I've found a way to convince Livio to let you go. The only thing is…he'll have to come down here."

He carried on despite the outburst from the unicorn.

"Listen to me. He only wants you to tell him that Castan isn't a threat. All you have to do is say that, and he'll free both of you. Convince him that all the power you can give him is through scrying, or prophecy, or something." Euphy drew on words he had learned from his days searching dictionaries to get Minari to agree. "And you won't ever have to think about him again."

"Whatever other capabilities I have, I am not an oracle."

"I know that, but Livio doesn't."

There was a long pause before Minari responded.

"Then I trust you. As my friend."

These were the words Euphy wanted to hear for the rest of his life, and for the first time, he could envision a world where he would get to.

When next he entered the stable, Livio walked beside him. Euphy's spirit soared with the knowledge that he and Minari would soon no longer be confined here, but he could hear Minari's restlessness within the pen. His breath came in huffs, and Euphy could see him trembling with the resentment he was suppressing.

"Unicorn," said Euphy in a voice that sounded falsely formal to his ear, but which he hoped would convince Livio

"Use your supernatural sight, and look into the prisoner Castan's heart. Can you tell us whether he's truly a threat to the king? Or whether the king should let him go?"

They had decided against saying that Castan fully supported Livio, since it wouldn't be believable even if a unicorn said it. But the point was to assure him that Castan wasn't actively planning anything.

"Though humans speak freely, they do not act easily," Minari answered with the words they had planned. "I do not sense that the prisoner in this castle is a threat to this king."

Minari recited the short speech perfectly, though Euphy knew how much it had cost him even to pretend to speak words of reassurance to Livio.

Livio stepped backward, breathless, as was usual for first encounter with a unicorn's presence.

"We must act quickly," he said. "The rebel will never change his heart. The sooner we show the world the error of such a way, the better off we'll be."

"That isn't...are you sure that's what he meant?" Euphy stammered. He tried to imagine where Livio had gotten this from. Could he have been so overwhelmed that he'd simply misunderstood the ringing words?

"I thought I heard something different. Didn't he say that the prisoner *wasn't* a threat?" he finished, careful not to reveal that he had understood perfectly well what Minari had said, or that he'd been the one who'd scripted it.

Livio looked at him sympathetically – almost apologetically.

"There are some things given to those born of nobility, which those who weren't so fortunate in their birth can't claim. And one of those is understanding the heart of someone else equally high-born. This creature and I, we are both on the same level. We understand each other in ways that I wouldn't expect you to comprehend."

From behind the bars, Minari snorted a curse.

"You see, he agrees with me," Livio said, proving that if he had understood Minari's words at all, he had no intention of telling the truth about it. Even someone who couldn't make out the exact words could easily have gathered the intent.

Euphy's could physically feel the anger emanating from Minari as Livio continued.

"I know it doesn't seem fair, and I wouldn't bring up any of these differences except in dire need. I don't want you to feel that I think any less of you for not being able to commune with it, or that your part in this is any less important. You did your best, and you brought me here. I wouldn't have been brave enough to try if it weren't for you."

"Liar!" Minari burst out, his head tossing dangerously.

But Euphy wasn't in a position to agree, not in front of Livio. He stood mute before both of them.

"I'm so sorry, but I haven't the time to explain this all to you now." Livio said, hastening away from him toward the stable's inner doors. "I must move quickly, but when I've taken care of this matter, we can talk again."

Euphy was left to stare disbelieving at the space where Livio had been. How had this plan, which had seemed so beautifully clear not one hour before, gone so wrong? How could Livio have been so shameless as to stand there and lie to both of their faces?

He blew out his breath and turned to Minari, expecting to confer on what their next move should be. But when he turned, Minari had fixed him with a glare that felt like looking into a setting sun.

"You brought that man here. You had me debase myself by speaking to him, and then you allowed him to take my words and twist them for his own purposes. You've allowed me to be used to further his evil, just as he wanted. If that rebel man dies, and Livio uses me as justification for it...I did what you asked because I trusted you, and *this* is what I've gotten for it? Why were you even with him in the first place? You've failed to answer me that."

"He summoned me. You were here when it happened. You know I had to go."

"But you've clearly been speaking with him since then. Have all of those been summons? Have you been selling me to him all this time?"

Never had Euphy so wanted to stay quiet, to walk away with his secrets and his friendship intact, but he'd never been able to resist when Minari asked him anything. Not since the very first day they'd met.

"It wasn't about you," he tried to explain. "He *thought* I was there to talk about you, but I wasn't. I went because…"

It sounded pathetic now to tell this noble creature that he'd first consorted with their enemy because he wanted to get revenge on Dandy, and because he lived in agony under the thought of losing Minari himself.

He believed that, in any other conditions, Minari would have understood. But he'd made the mistake of trusting his heart to a friend under strained conditions before, and if a mere man had trampled it so easily, how much more capable would a unicorn be of doing the same?

"I couldn't fix my problem with Dandy; you remember the one I told you about? I thought Livio might be able to help."

"And this problem was worth going to that devil? You couldn't have settled it any other way? You couldn't handle it yourself with the advice I gave you?"

"No, I couldn't handle it. We can't all be as strong as you," Euphy shot back. He'd been right in thinking Minari wouldn't understand.

"Did you even try?" Minari's voice was rising to that shrillness which always preceded his terrible trumpeting shriek. The same one Minari had used to keep Dandy from getting too close. Dandy – the person he was now admonishing Euphy for having trouble with.

What a hypocrite.

Crimson fingertips of indignation curled themselves between Euphy's teeth, prying his mouth open.

"You didn't like Dandy so much yourself when you saw him," he reminded Minari. "He tried to come in here once, to use you for *his* own gain, and you ran him off. How can you scold me for doing the same?

"Because *I* have not chosen to go to Livio. *I* have not been sharing information about someone who thought of me as a friend. What else did you tell him? Did you share – ?"

Euphy knew what Minari had stopped short of saying.

"What do you think?" he cried. It didn't matter whether he had actually shared Minari's precious name with Livio or not. If Minari *thought* he did, if he even thought that Euphy *would*, it would be equally humiliating, and every bit as heartbreaking.

"You let yourself be charmed by him, you foolish boy! You swallowed every one of his lies, and you've ruined us all. Better that I had never met you, than to have you betray my life to him like this."

How could Minari hold a frail human to a standard that even a beast of fantastica could not meet?

"In case you've forgotten, even *you* weren't able to resist him, when he wanted you." Euphy was near shouting now, matching Minari's wild pitch. "That's why you're here in the first place, isn't it? At least I have the excuse of being a foolish human. What about you, with all your grand claims of wisdom, and your stupid white coat? What a lie to say that unicorns have to be wise to get to be your color. Anyone that wise wouldn't let themselves be captured in the first place.

I'd be ashamed to be as old as you, and letting myself get snared like that. And to be so useless that I had to depend on a 'foolish boy' to take care of me. Though I have to say, the most foolish thing I ever did was waste so much time on *you*."

Euphy's chest heaved from the force of the words, and he waited for the recoil, terrible and magnificent, which he knew must be coming.

But none came. The shimmer of Minari's hide, which had flared to a hectically bright shade as they'd traded accusations, dimmed down to a sickly flicker, and he turned away.

He looked just as he did in the days before he and Euphy had been friends, and it yanked Euphy back to his senses. This was the one creature he'd give anything to stay beside, and *that* was all he could think to say to him? All the work he had done to return Minari to his rightful grandeur, and the second Minari acted accordingly, Euphy had torn him down again.

"I didn't – " He choked on the words he'd intended to say, but swallowed and tried again.

"You know I…" The words still failed to come.

He was supposed to be Minari's defender. The one who would keep him safe from anyone who would hurt him, but he had become just like Dandy, slinging painful words at a vulnerable heart who had trusted in him.

I'm sorry.

He would say it a hundred times over if it meant that Minari would glow that beautiful bright white again. If he would only *look* at him again.

He could have screamed for how desperately he wanted to apologize, but his mouth outright refused to form the words. For all the times Euphy had been unable to stay silent in Minari's presence, this was the one time the spell had failed him.

"Don't speak to me ever again." Minari's voice was black and empty. "Don't come near me at all. You were right about one thing. I was foolish to have trusted you."

"But I have to look after you. If I don't come…"

"Then I'll die and be out of my misery, where none of you can presume upon me anymore."

When Minari had first come to the dungeon, he'd looked listless and grey, but he'd still had fight in his words. His voice had been steel and fire even when his body had been water and ice. He had refused to admit that he was anything less than the same mighty force of nature that he'd been in the wilds, or acknowledge the fact that he was in danger of anything like dying. Out of all the frightening things Minari had ever done, for him to be speaking of death like this, to be wishing for it, was the worst of them all.

Euphy tried once more to force his apology out, digging his fingernails into his palms until he felt the skin breaking, but even this blood sacrifice was not enough to appease the twin gods of shame and pride that kept his tongue in their hands.

With a sob, all the expression that was afforded his regret, he turned and fled from the pen, the same way so many had gone before him – Stregatto, Dandy, and Livio had all run from Minari in the same manner. It was apparently the way of cruel men unworthy to be in Minari's presence.

Euphy knew he no longer had to fear the day when Vanya would claim Minari and carry him away to where Euphy could not reach. Because in the end, Euphy had lost Minari all by himself.

*   *   *

For once in his life, Euphy wished Dario would come back from the market, to order him back into Minari's pen. But Dario hadn't returned; Euphy figured that the punishment for Castan was being publicly announced, and that Dario was probably busy railing against it amongst his fellow patriots.

So Euphy sat with his back against the stable's interior doors, staring into the dark corridor, lit dimly by torchlight, which led to the upper levels. He couldn't stay in the stable now, but he couldn't bear to be away from it, so he'd settled for sitting just on the other side of the doors.

His knees were pulled up to his chest, and from the darkness came the unwelcome taunting voice which somehow showed up like clockwork every time something was going wrong with Minari.

"Sleeping in the dirt this time, are you? And during working hours, too. You really do resemble those animals of yours."

"Just tell me what you want," Euphy groaned. Was Stregatto at all capable of getting to the point without having to go through these irritating little opening remarks first?

"I'm here for the beast."

"Keep on dreaming," said Euphy. He felt the quick pull of tension in his bones, but he wasn't going to show that to Stregatto.

"Watch out, boy. Remember what happened the last time you mouthed off to me. You might get away with it in front of Livio, but that's why he has people like me, to do the heavy lifting."

"You're not taking the unicorn."

"You didn't mind dangling the chance to have him in front of the king as long as it got you free privileges, did you? If you didn't want to give him up, you shouldn't have pretended like you did. Not that it would've kept His Highness from getting what he wanted, but you wouldn't have looked so two-faced in front of him."

Something told Euphy that this wasn't just Stregatto talking. It was how Livio really felt about him. And the stupidest thing was, Euphy had known it from the start.

He had gone into this arrangement thinking to outsmart Livio, to outclass Dandy, and assumed that nobody else but him had a hand to play.

But Livio's iron hand held more cards than Euphy had guessed, and he'd spun Euphy around to exactly where he'd wanted him.

Livio treated Euphy as a friend, as an honored guest, as someone worthy of time and attention. And Euphy, like a fool, had fallen under the glamour of this fey king, had come dancing every time he was called. And he had thought *he'd* been the one in control all the while.

But the truth was, he'd been tamed like any dog, and was now expected to roll over and take Livio's abuse like one. He was being expected to hand his treasured Minari over to his master as a dog would give up a bone. And Euphy was certain that if he ever saw Livio's face again, it would wear that same wounded look and pretend not to know what he was upset about, and pretend to be hurt by any accusation Euphy made.

Shame rushed its well-worn course through him, sending him leaping to his feet. "I've told you before. If Livio wants him, he can come down here himself, and stop relying on you to do his dirty work."

"Dirty work, huh?" Stregatto repeated. "Sounds like you've finally gotten it about right. I don't know what game you thought we were all playing, but it was always going to end this way. The beast was always for Livio, and it was always my job to make sure you'd appreciate that in the end. Or did you think we'd brought it here as a pet for you?

You're dumb animals, both of you, but I've dealt with dumb animals before." He shook himself as if to limber his muscles for some great exertion.

It looked like the picture in *Research in Fantastica* of a werebeast rising up in front of a full moon. Was this what Minari had seen the night he'd been taken? Had he known that at the end of it would be a pit of darkness below leagues of stone while a pretender with a delicate face and a deceitful heart sprawled carelessly amidst swirls of light in airy halls above?

Had Minari felt this same red rage at the hulking shadow before him?

Euphy collided with Stregatto the way he would have collided with a brick wall. But unlike a brick wall, Stregatto was surprised by his initiative. Not much, but just enough.

They ended on the ground, with Euphy on Stregatto's back with his elbows hooked around Stregatto's throat, knowing the odds of successfully finishing this were low, and not caring.

Stregatto had been strong enough to take the mighty Minari captive, but Euphy hadn't been the unicorn's guardian then, and he would not let this grinning cat of a man touch Minari again, no matter what else happened.

And a man doesn't break horses for twenty years without gaining some strength of his own.

He forced Stregatto's chin up with his forearm. "I'll kill you before I let that happen," he swore, and meant it.

Finally, Stregatto managed to toss Euphy forward over his shoulder, but Euphy sprang up again, undaunted, until he saw behind Stregatto another of the hunters, Corvin, who was bigger and looked stronger than even Stregatto. He had his arms folded, but appeared impressed rather than angered by Euphy's behavior.

"Come, Stregatto. We're needed outside," he said, but he kept his eyes on Euphy.

"It's my job to make sure the unicorn is ready to serve the king," Stregatto argued.

"You don't have to tell me," Corvin said. "But you can do that better by clearing a whole mob out of the way than just one person. It's more exciting out there besides."

He looked at Euphy as they turned to leave. "I like your spirit. Not many would challenge Stregatto like that, nor last so long against him. Keep yourself on the right side of all this, and you'll likely keep your place when it's done. His Majesty will always need someone to keep his unicorn in top form."

Euphy was too used to empty praise, and too disgusted by Minari being called "Livio's unicorn" to be swayed by the compliment. He was ready to attack the hunters' disappearing forms again, but if he went after them, he'd be further away from Minari, which would leave him without protection if anyone else came for him.

Both he and Minari had been out-maneuvered by Livio and his followers before. The first instance had brought them together. The second one had torn them apart. Euphy would not let there be a third time.

CHAPTER 21
Dear Fellow Traveller

Bridle worried about the four in the castle – Castan, Euphy, Dandy, and the unicorn – all through the long day. But he still had to draw up plans of attack, and tried to ignore these thoughts as drew up plans for how the rebel forces should position themselves across the market at the hanging. He remembered how he and Euphy had run through the wheel-spoke streets of the market, all the corners and turns, all the potential trouble spots where they could lose an advantage.

He listed these out to the four dancers who stood before him now – Gioa, Lazaro, Serena, and Beria – who were to form an advance party, a small group who would attempt to save Castan by stealth before the larger force took action. A group that size could move faster and attract less attention, and if they were successful, they would save the rest of the troupe from revealing their true numbers too soon.

Bridle instructed them not to run toward the encircling alley, thinking of how Dandy had cut the young thief off at every pass. He also remembered how easy it had been for Dandy, who was just one man. There would be more than one waiting for them this time, and he bit his lip to keep from showing his fear of it to the dancers who were at last becoming soldiers before him.

Bridle had never before doubted his own ability to put anyone exactly where they needed to go, but now he felt that even his best plans wouldn't be enough. Everything Castan said about him – how his skills weren't ready for a real test – was coming true just as Castan was on the way to his grave.

Next, the captains called in their squadrons one-by-one, explaining the all-too-fragile plan to each of them. It was more time-consuming than doing it in muster formation, but it was also less likely to be overheard by anyone outside the camp.

Through these long hours, Bridle kept his feet, standing between Emmanuel and Golden. Mechanically, he repeated where each squadron was to go, what they were to do, but his mind was filled with images of Castan swinging in the background of the battle, and of Livio, unstoppable with stolen strength from the unicorn, emerging from the castle to cut down all opposition.

And Dandy? Euphy? Where would they be in all of this? Was Euphy somewhere worrying over his creature the same way Bridle was fretting over Castan? They both had someone they cared about held captive by Livio.

Or what if he and Dandy had been found out as rebels? Was that the reason why they'd remained absent as the day crawled on?

Bridle hadn't thought the image of Castan at the end of a rope could become any more ghastly until it transformed into three figures above a scaffold, casting their swaying shadows on the conflict.

"Ma'am?" asked one of Vitalia's dancers, when she had paused in her speech to them. "Is it true? That Livio took the unicorn's sight, and that's how he knew who Castan was?"

"How can we fight against the king now that he's got a unicorn's power? Won't it – ?"

"No need to worry," Vitalia cut him off. "We know what we're doing, and that's all you need to think on. If you do that, it'll be over before you even notice any unicorn power."

Bridle privately thought that if he had been the one asking the question, this wouldn't have reassured him much, but as of now, they didn't have any other plan. They had to go ahead with it, even if it killed them.

It was all the more bitter because Bridle knew that in any other circumstance, he could have come up with ten good ideas in short order, ten adjustments that might give them even a shade more of a chance. But the dread that had stayed with him since he'd met the woman at the well kept his mind an icy blank.

By evening, even after the captains had gone to bed with bleak expressions, Bridle was the only one left in the Command Room besides Golden, who watched him as he pored once more over their battle plans, unable to persuade himself that any of them would work.

Bridle pressed his hand to his forehead, trying to force his thoughts into order. "Are you sure we can't go *find* Euphy? Ask him how we could get around the unicorn's power?" he suggested.

"However dangerous it was this morning, it will be doubly so tonight, especially if Livio really has that power by now. And anyway, the castle doors will be locked by this time. Or they always were when I was there."

"If Dandy were here, he could have seen the way through this," he muttered for what was not the first time that day.

Golden looked sympathetic but said nothing. He had, of course been informed of Dandy's contributions up until now, but he hadn't seen Dandy himself, or known just how brilliant, how inspiring the person of Dandy could be. Of course he wouldn't feel the absence of such a force as keenly as everyone else did, thought Bridle.

"You should try to get some sleep," Golden offered finally. "You've drawn up a good plan. You couldn't have done better under the circumstances."

Bridle looked up at him, the furrow in his brow deepening, and he shook his head. He knew no sleep would come to him now.

"You have to try," Golden pressed again. "If we go to war tomorrow, you'll need all of your strength."

"If…" Bridle sighed. "Isn't there any other way? Do we really have to offer half of ourselves to be slaughtered just so that *some* of us might make it through?"

Vanya knew that even in his distress, Bridle's mind was too sharp not to see that this plan, as painful was it was, made the most logistical sense. He also knew that an understanding of the concept would do nothing to help him be at peace with it.

Anyone involved in a mission like theirs would know that there was an element of loss involved, but for all that Bridle had been helping to plan a revolution, it seemed that he hadn't fully realized what the consequences of one would be. In his mind, they would have seemed like some distant thing, which, by a vague notion of luck or providence, would touch only the enemy and not him.

This Vanya knew because had once been the same way. He'd been trained, clearly effectively, on how to handle a sword, but he hadn't thought about what it would really mean to take one in hand until the moment he'd been forced to do it.

Now it was Bridle's unfortunate privilege to go through the same experience. This would be his first exposure to the fact that the world could take things from him, that people he cared about could actually get hurt.

Vanya saw in Bridle's unease the same doubts, the same endless questions which he'd asked himself all through his exile:

"If I had been stronger, smarter, could I have prevented this?…What's wrong with me that I'm so frightened by what I have to do?…If the person I depended on is gone, can I make it on my own without him?"

174

"Try to put those thoughts from your mind," Vanya said. "I know it feels like wisdom to consider them, but they're lying to you. You can trust me on that."

Bridle's head snapped toward him. The acknowledgement of the fears that he was sure were his alone, that he couldn't show to anyone else, abruptly cracked the wall he'd been desperately holding up against them, and in an instant, he was giving voice to every fatal image, all of the worries, doubts, and hopeless reflections – naming each of the dark, shifting shadows leering at him from the corners of his sight, daring him to turn his head and look at the horror of their faces.

Vanya was not surprised by any of them. They were the same ghosts that had haunted him for twenty years, and he saw that they had no intention of leaving now, not when they had the chance to crush what Livio had failed to kill the first time he'd attacked Ausonia.

Back then, Vanya had no foreknowledge of what he would have to do. Abandoning his father hadn't crossed his mind until the very moment it became necessary. He hadn't had to fear it before it happened.

It was terrible now to *know* that they might have to abandon Castan. But something else was different this time, too. This time, Vanya had Bridle and all the others depending on him. It was his own worst fear coming to pass, but he found to his amazement that this moment filled him not with anguish, but assurance.

Because he had someone else to care for, he had no time to focus on himself. By tending to the others, he could block out the voices whispering calamity to him. By focusing on his little lambs instead of on himself, something of that old fire which had carried him through the Night of New Glory had sputtered back to life.

There was something still in his heart which was able to rise to necessity, despite what the demons had told him for twenty years.

He put a hand on Bridle's shoulder. "We'll help each other not to pay attention to them. How does that sound?"

He didn't tell Bridle not to cry as the younger man hung his head. He had shed enough tears throughout his own life to know the futility of such words.

"Castan and the others aren't gone from us yet. There are things left which we can do for them. You must think on that, otherwise you won't be able to do those things when the time comes."

The despairing person who could not see any light in the future was who Vanya had been, but not who he had to be now. The darkness he had walked through had taught him the lessons he needed to become Prince Vanya again, but it no longer had to define him.

He folded his arms around Bridle, who was by now openly sobbing.

Livio might have the unicorn, but Vanya had the ability, hard won by years of suffering, to shine a light on the way of someone wandering in the wilderness, to help a young man facing a flood of dark waters learn how to keep his head above them.

How glad he was now that he'd been learning this ability all the while he'd been travelling alone, even without knowing that he *was* learning it, so that he could make the way easier for those coming behind him.

All the years he had spent out in the harsh world, the years which he'd considered such a waste, were revealing themselves all at once to have had their purpose. They had been difficult and lonely, but without them, he would never have been able to see things from the other side. He would still be a sheltered, ignorant princeling, knowing nothing even forty four years on from his birth, and the innocence which had always seemed to Vanya like a tragically lost jewel would now be a handicap that rendered him more unfit for reality than anything else he had faced.

If it meant he could rescue Bridle, and all the Ausonians who were depending on him, from the same fate he'd met, then it was worth every minute of pain he'd gone through. But it would not serve anyone if he were to keep living in that pain for a minute longer. In this night which should have been darkest, Vanya could finally see the way forward.

*   *   *

Streaks of sunlight crept over Bridle's face. It was the wan, weak sunlight of winter, but Bridle felt unaccountably warmed by it. His back ached and his cheeks were stiff with dried salt, but the crushing dread of the past day didn't seem to weigh on him as heavily. He couldn't remember why, until he noticed Golden near him, on no more exalted a bed than the dirt floor of the Command Room, and he remembered the torrent of tears and the strong support of Golden's shoulder.

Bridle had plenty of experience sleeping on the ground while he minded sheep in the night, but for a prince to have to do it made Bridle a little sorry, though it was comfort to think that he had gained so kind and capable a shepherd of his own to be watched over by.

And capable Vanya was, Bridle thought, wondering how he could ever have doubted the power of this golden prince, who saw into men's hearts, who carried magic in his hands, and cast out devils by the gentleness of his words.

Vanya stirred and sat up more gracefully than someone who had slept in the dirt had any right to.

"Sorry," Bridle said. "I didn't mean to make you stay here with me all night."

"I wouldn't have deserted you," Vanya said. "Besides, I've slept in worse accommodations than this."

"I guess we'd better get up. Today is… well, there's a lot to be done today, and I'd hate to go into it without even washing my face."

"Will you be alright?"

"I will if you're with us."

"I wouldn't desert you," Vanya said again.

"Then let's go."

CHAPTER 22
White Waves

Castan looked out at the crowd before the scaffold. At least half of them looked back at him with sympathetic faces, but that was little comfort when four other morrismen stood next to him.

The group had tried and failed to free him as he'd been led from Prisma to Clockface, and had earned themselves their own places on the scaffold.

Gioa, in spite of the beating that she'd taken from the guards, kept her chin raised proudly as she stared down the crowd, challenging them to pity or scorn her. Pious Lazaro's lips moved in prayer, and Serena's nimble fingers, which were supposed to have picked the locks of Castan's cuffs, twisted to find any weakness in the knots of her bonds. Meanwhile, Beria taunted the guard who held her, telling him to stand up straight and pointing out that he had wrinkles in his Livian grey uniform.

And all of them were pretending that they didn't know Castan, for to admit that they'd had a personal stake in his fate, that they'd been advised to do it by any person or force aside from their own personal opposition to Livio, would give their enemy the very answer he was looking for.

Only one scaffold had been built, so the five would have to go one at a time. Castan was to be first, so that the others could die with their eyes full of the sight they had vainly forfeited their lives to prevent.

The process of the hanging was slow and tedious. It opened with a lengthy speech reminding everyone about Livio's greatness and glory, and Castan almost found himself wishing that the orator would hurry up – until he remembered what waited at the end of this speech.

Next came the predictable nonsense, just like at every other hanging, about this being the last chance for the traitors to acknowledge the truth of what had been said, and renounce their stance against Livio.

"That's not a thing to be renounced or given up, any more than I can renounce my own skin," Castan answered.

"You'll be deprived of that soon enough," was the orator's curt reply. It was a break in the officious, droning tone he'd been using all morning, at any rate.

"*Nothing like a little variety before dying,*" Castan thought.

Finally, he was pushed forward to the noose. The hooded man at the lever which would release the floor from under him asked if he had any final statement to make before the end.

"Would've liked to see the sea," Castan muttered, looking at the sky, which was the closest thing to it that he could imagine.

There were so many things that he'd planned to do…and all of them *after*. After the pressing needs of life had been dealt with, after he'd taken care of Golden, after helping him reclaim his rightful home.

Not that he regretted the things he'd done. Everything he'd done for Golden, he'd do again. But just because he'd had wishes for someone else didn't mean he could entirely forget the ones he'd once held for himself.

And it was such a simple wish. Compared to all the other things, the important things – just to see the wide, shining blue, with white caps breaking its surface – could he be faulted for cherishing this humble fantasy?

He saw them in his mind now, rising above the assembly. But after a moment, it became clear that the forms rising up from the crowd weren't in his imagination, but rather actual depictions of a white waves on pennants of blue – the banners of King Nereus, raised by figures in black.

Unlike the first half of the hanging, so much about the scene that followed was swift, and not at all usual. Other hangings didn't usually involve a collective shout breaking out before the accused had even been killed, or the spectators thronging around a figure who wore the face of one already dead – Nereus's son, revealed like a vengeful spirit in their midst.

Other hangings did not involve Serena working her bonds loose and kicking her personal guard over the edge of the platform, down to the oncoming surge, before turning and freeing Beria next to her, which was an admirable feat given that Beria was herself already battling with her own guard, using everything but her hands.

When Beria was free, the two of them together flung her guard downward, and she flew toward Castan to defend him while Serena worked on Lazaro.

Members of the crowd who had already reached the scaffold swarmed up the steps as Lazaro, who did not believe that piety was the same thing as pacifism, slammed his big shoulder into the nearest guard, then wrenched the pike from the guard's shock-loosened fingers and flipped it deftly down and into the man's throat. Gioa, who'd been liberated by someone from the crowd, came alongside him, to help cover for Serena as she finally worked on Castan's ties.

Through the clouds of conflict, Bridle came bounding, pushing past both of them to throw his arms around Castan. Though it was for no more than an instant – any longer would have been unwise in the current situation – Bridle looked as if the battle had been won right then.

"Let's get you out of here," he said, sounding happier than he'd ever sounded when addressing Castan before.

"It'd be nice if I had my gloves "

Bridle pulled a pair of brass-knuckled gloves from where they were tied to his waist and shoved them toward Castan, who pulled them on with practiced ease, and hands that remembered the time before he'd had a prince to care for, the days when he'd scrapped for sport to earn his living, and beaten and bloodied men in exchange for a day's wages.

He'd hated it at the time, but those days stood him in good stead now. He instinctively knew when to feint, when to attack, and when to reach over and grab the arm of Bridle beside him, pulling him out of the way of an enemy strike.

But for all these little victories, there was not as much progress as Castan would have liked.

"What's the plan?" he called to Bridle beside him. "We going forward?"

"All the way to Prisma. Golden's orders."

"You sure they're not just luring us in, to trap us in their defended ground?"

"Of course they are, but we've already played our hand. We retreat now, and we'd have to fight our way back here again. No use in re-doing progress we've already made."

"You really did think of everything. Golden was right to listen to you."

Bridle was in the process of elbowing an Albionite in the face, but was nonetheless able to feel the compliment. Castan was finally acknowledging his value, but Bridle couldn't begrudge him the tardiness of the realization. Not after having been so late in learning Castan's value himself. If it had cost Castan anything like what it had cost him, that would be chastisement enough.

And so they advanced, side by side through the Livian forces, making their way to Golden, who had once divided them. But now, as they approached the end of the journey that had started as a small, weak hope years ago, they were of the same mind at last.

Small and weak their hope may have been, but at least they held onto it together.

CHAPTER 23
Though Envious Years
Would Say Forget

Dandy's window faced to the west, where the market and its gallows lay. By tomorrow, he would no longer look out of this window. By tomorrow, Castan might be dead.

He packed only a few small remnants of the life he could no longer bear to lead – he had neither the time nor the wish to take anything else. Most of the luxury he'd been used to had come from Livio's hand, and he refused to take anything with that stain on it into his new life. He did take his sword, though. That had been his own from the beginning, and he would make it atone for the service it had once given to the false king.

It swung reassuringly in its sheath as he made his way to the last remaining value which Prisma Castle held for him. He still didn't know how he was going to explain the situation to Theodora, but having his sword by his side made him feel better.

He'd entertained visions of barricading her door from the inside, of sleeping on her threshold in case anyone came for in the night, but all of this would mean that he was making the decision for her.

His old self would have said that these reservations were ridiculous, and gone ahead with his plans. But his old self had never come face to face with a serious man whose eyes performed an inquisition on everyone they met, and found himself entirely lacking. His old self would have been the one coming to take her.

He ended up spending the night with his back against an alcove near her room, only half-sleeping, with his hand on his sword – near enough to help if he were needed, but far enough not to be seen if he weren't wanted, if she chose to go with Livio when he came for her.

Though when the morning came and Livio hadn't, Dandy knew that this limbo couldn't hold. He had to say something to Theodora, to at least explain what was happening. He could do that without telling her how to feel about it, but he couldn't spend the rest of his life waiting outside of her door.

Just as he'd knocked on the familiar wood panel, the distant sound of shouts reached him. They were faint cries, carried in through the corridor's open lancet windows, obviously from some distance.

It wasn't unusual for crowds to raise a cry when an execution ultimately came to its conclusion, but Dandy knew the sounds of conflict too well not to recognize them for what they were.

The morrismen must have finally decided to move, to rise up in response to Castan's hanging. Dandy's conscience stung, knowing that he wasn't with them.

Theodora opened the door herself, surprised to see Dandy with his hands on the nearest window frame.

"What's the matter?" she asked.

Dandy could see a mass of forms on the green field, pressing up the road toward the castle. Figures scattered across the green were joining them, and above it all, specks of blue and silver streamed in the wind.

Dandy squinted, trying to see more clearly. Those were the banners of Nereus, that Dandy had once seen atop the castle, when he'd been the one advancing on it with the intent to topple everything inside.

In all the time spent planning this moment, Dandy had never intended that it would happen with himself and Theodora inside. He'd planned to be out there, marching as he had once before, to overthrow the king in Prisma.

He turned from the window. There would no longer be any time to explain things to Theodora at all. He had get her to safety first; he could tell her the details later.

If they waited, they would be stuck inside when the battle arrived, and though the morrismen might recognize him, there was no guarantee that they wouldn't fight against him. Who knew what Euphy had told them by now? And if they were frenzied enough by Castan's hanging to launch their full assault like this, they might just be willing to repay Dandy for his lies at the same time.

With a clarity that always came to him when a battle was in the air, he saw that standing here wishing he'd done things differently was the least effective thing he could do. He shoved his regrets aside and took Theodora's wrist.

"Dandy, what's happening?"

"Just a little excitement," he said, taking her arm and trying to sound nonchalant even as people were beginning to rush past them, and the distinct sounds of metal on metal began to be discernible through the windows.

She obediently followed him, though he felt her fingers tightening around his arm as he led her through the corridors and down the winding stairs, keeping up a stream of chatter to distract her, and to distract himself from the thought that this must have been how she had felt and looked on the Night of New Glory. That battle had turned her into what she was now. How much more damage would this next one do?

"You know that sometimes the military has to practice," he was saying as they neared the stable. "It doesn't mean anything is –"

He was cut off by a rolling boom so loud that Theodora screamed and Dandy stumbled. He reaching out to steady her, but she reeled away until her back hit the wall, and she leaned hard against it, eyes closed and hands on her forehead.

Dandy stepped toward her, but a second blast followed and Theodora screamed again, twisting against the wall as if trying to make it absorb her. Her shoulders heaved and she started clawing her hands through her hair.

"We've have to keep going," Dandy said as calmly as he could, though he had to raise his voice to be heard above her cries.

"Don't touch me," she shrieked.

"It's alright to be afraid, but I'll take care of you. We'll just go on a little journey," he said, as if this "little journey" were not going to be a desperate flight through an active battle.

He took her hand and resumed his flight, jogging now toward the stable. Theodora was resisting him, pulling back against his lead like a fearful horse refusing to move.

"We'll be fine. Come along," he coaxed, but she pulled back harder, wrenching her arm free from his grasp with a fierce look.

"I won't go with you!" she cried, and Dandy himself felt a wave of fear pass over him. It seemed the thing he had dreaded had finally come to pass –

this second conflict had finally broken her mind to the point where she no longer recognized him.

"You're not safe here. I won't hurt you, but the people who are coming for us might, if you stay." To the morrismen, Theodora would look like any other lady of the court. They would have no way of knowing she was Nereus's daughter.

"If my castle is under attack, I have to defend it. So unless you're taking me to the armory, you'll please not force me anywhere."

Even on her worst days, she had been quiet and serene, but she declared this now with sharpness and determination. Was this the next stage in her descent toward a total loss of sanity – that she would go from a gentle unawareness of the world's dangers to a reckless disregard of them?

"You must listen to me. How could you?"

"How could I what? Defend the castle? Use my two hands to pick up a weapon and point it at somebody, the same as anyone else."

Dandy stared at her. There was something more to this than simple ignorance. She spoke not like a dreaming madwoman, but like a true princess. Like she knew exactly what she was saying, and knew that she had the authority to do it.

He looked at the proud carriage of her head, her clear eyes, and the way her shoulders were thrown back in defiance, and it came to him that this was not his first great fear coming true, but his second. It wasn't that she had failed to recognize him. It was that she had succeeded.

He tried to open his mouth, and couldn't. I almost felt like when he had approached the unicorn. If he dared say anything to her, he felt that she would cut him in half where he stood. Or else she would call him exactly what he was and banish him from her presence, which would be the same thing.

He had been right about what this battle would do to her. It *had* changed her, but instead of sending her further into herself, it had rattled the bonds loose which had caged her for so long.

"Do you remember?" he finally asked.

"Yes, I remember," she said, each word a knife point. "That night. All of it."

Dandy held his breath, waiting to hear her destroy him.

But then her face changed.

"I remember everything that happened after that night, too. You needn't be so worried. It's alright."

She was looking at him as if he were a helpless animal in need of her protection. It came to him that this was probably the way he'd always looked at her.

"Come with me, then," he breathed. How inconvenient that his heart should start that lovestruck pounding when there were more pressing matters, like the battle bearing down on them right at this moment.

"My father and brother are gone," she replied in quiet apology. "I have to finish it. I have to do what they couldn't."

"It's not from the people out there that you'll need to defend yourself. The true Ausonians – the ones who would support you – are the ones attacking the castle now. But if you go out there, they won't recognize you for who you are. All they'll see is a court lady, and they'll likely attack you as soon as help you. Nobody out there even knows you're alive."

"Then I'll make myself useful some other way. I can distract—oh, what's his name? The one who took my father's crown?"

"You mean Livio?"

She laughed, a strangely bright sound in the war-heavy atmosphere. "Well, perhaps I don't remember *everything* just yet."

"You don't intend…to become his bride?"

"Certainly not," she made a face at him.

"Then what will you do?" The brave general could not bring himself to speak the words out loud, to ask whether she would have him in place of Livio.

"Right now, I'm going to help win this battle in whatever way I can. "

The floor beneath them shook.

"Go to them. Help them fight," she said.

"I won't leave you if you need me."

How wonderful it was to be able to ask Theodora her own mind, to know that she could decide for herself what she needed, even if that didn't include him.

"I *have* needed you," she said. "Even when I didn't know all that you were really doing for me, I needed you. But I won't hold you back anymore. It's time for you to go and do what you were meant to."

His pounding heart warmed to know that she really had come to know him somewhere in the locked corners of her mind. But there was no time to focus on that now.

"You know how to get somewhere safe on your own?" he asked.

"I'll be fine. You've made sure of that. Other people need your help now."

He took her hands. How ironic that she had come back into awareness of the world just as it was about to crumble away. That she could smile at him just as he was on the brink of having to leave her forever.

"If I survive," he said, "I'll come back."

He took one labored step forward and touched her face, then suddenly decisively, he pulled her to him, hoping that the pounding in chest would communicate to her what his mouth could not, until he was sure that if he stayed there for one moment longer, he would lose the will to let her go again.

Without giving himself time to second-guess, he leaned down, kissed her forehead, then turned and fled toward the stable and the green field beyond.

CHAPTER 24
Hearken Then, Ere Voice of Dread

"So much for Dandy the Morningstar," a mocking voice came from the shadows just before Dandy reached the stable doors, and Euphy stepped out before him.

He must have observed the whole scene from the darkness, and Dandy's embarrassment fought with relief at seeing him here, safe from what was happening outside. With all the hurt they had put each other through, ("*And most of that coming from my side*," Dandy reflected), he did not want to see Euphy suffer any more.

But why *was* Euphy here, and not helping the rebels? Had he truly gone over to Livio's side?

Dandy asked him what his purpose was, and Euphy cracked a feral grin, looking almost like one of Livio's hunters.

"It's not making eyes at noble ladies, that's for sure," he said. "Why are *you* here? If you're coming for the unicorn, I can't let that happen. I won't let you use him the same way you use everyone else."

He put a hand on his hip, where Dandy could see a shortsword barely glinting in the shadows.

"It's not me who needs him," said Dandy. "Castan and all of our friends are out there fighting, maybe dying, if they haven't already. Couldn't you give the unicorn up for that? Or are you here because *Livio*'s told you not to let anyone take him?"

"I'm not here to do anything for anyone. Not for Livio, not for you, and not for the morrismen, either. You're all the same; all any of you care about is how you can use the unicorn to get your chosen one on the throne. None of you care about him for who he is. You don't know anything about him, but you're all trying to make him your own personal tool."

Dandy felt his ire wanting to rise, but he clamped his teeth shut. He'd been speechless only a few minutes ago with Theodora; he could force himself to remain so, and avoid saying the sort of thing he would have said when he was the Morningstar. The sort of thing which had driven Euphy to Livio in the first place.

But what was Euphy planning to do, if he no longer trusted neither Livio nor Castan's forces? Did he imagine that he could fight both sides off at the same time? He was valiant. Dandy wouldn't argue against that.

"How can I get you to trust me? Would it help if I stayed here, defended him with you?"

"I wouldn't trust you any nearer him than the rest."

"Maybe not, but the rest will be here soon, and if you really want to protect your unicorn, you'd better be with him." Dandy spoke from his own experience with Theodora. "Waiting out here in the shadows isn't going to do much for him when the fight comes in from the field."

The walls shook again, but Euphy stayed where he was.

With a sinking feeling, Dandy saw that he would have to *make* Euphy move.

He'd been fortunate with Theodora. She had understood all that he'd meant to say, and forgiven

194

him all the things he hadn't been able to ask for. But it was clear that Euphy could not.

Dandy would have to find his bravery, to be able to say what Euphy needed to hear, if either of them were ever going leave this spot.

He said Euphy's name, hearing the tremor in his own voice, but pushed ahead. "I've wronged you. I admit that now, and...I'm asking you to forgive me. The words, unused to them as he was, weren't nearly so difficult to say as he'd expected. He'd said them enough times in his heart, it turned out that saying them with his mouth wasn't much different, in the end.

The savagery of Euphy's expression wavered in the shadows, but he didn't answer.

"Imagine how your unicorn feels. In there alone without you who were supposed to watch out for him."

"You think I don't know that? But I can't go back to him. Not now," Euphy started with a snap, but his voice quickly dwindled, and he hardly seemed to remember whom he was talking to as he finished. "I'm the one who's hurt him the worst. I've said things...done things...and I don't have the right to go near him now."

"Then let me help you," Dandy reached out toward him.

"Don't!" Euphy cried, bringing his blade up, but Dandy, by long-practiced reflex, parried and knocked it to the floor. Into the emptiness of Euphy's palm, he thrust his own gloved hand, and the grip that remembered how to hold a sword now stilled Euphy's trembling.

"If you have anything to repent of, I have more. I don't think even *you* would argue with that," he said, and Euphy managed a suffocated gasp of a laugh.

"I know how easy it is to lose sight of yourself in Livio's shadow, but you don't have to stay there.

Neither of us do. I'll walk with you, if you'll walk with me."

The rumbling outside grew louder. Euphy still didn't respond, but at least he hadn't withdrawn his hand.

The noise of the battle was beckoning Dandy, and he longed to run toward it, though he would not move before Euphy did, no matter what the cost. If he were to take even one step, everything they'd gained here would be undone. Even if it meant winning the battle, if he were to drag Euphy from this spot before he was ready, if he were to once again impose his will on the man he'd driven here by his own self-importance, it would shatter every chance for Euphy to return to himself.

He knew what it was to realize that you were not the person you thought you were, and what it was to realize that you could still *become* the person you wanted to be, starting by *choosing* to act as that person. And so he must let Euphy be the one who chose to take the first step back to the unicorn.

If Euphy had caused a separation between them, he must also be the one to initiate its healing, or he would never believe in his own power to do it, and with the battle bearing down on them, it might his last time to try.

Euphy took several labored breaths, his face an echo of what Theodora's had been as her memories had come back to her, until with one final, determined exhalation, he set his shoulders and looked at Dandy.

"This doesn't mean that I trust you," he said, and gripped Dandy's hand tightly as he stepped forward. "But if I have to take you with me, then let's go."

So Dandy hadn't yet succeeded in earning Euphy's forgiveness. But Euphy was walking, was holding onto him, and that was progress. Down to the lonely world beneath the castle where a white fire flickered in solitude, they walked side by side.

Dandy could feel Euphy stiffening as the oaken doors loomed before them. But Euphy steadfastly kept his widening eyes forward, and together they pushed the doors open without speaking.

The hinges wailed into the silence. Rows of tack hung in disarray and stalls stood empty where horses had already been saddled and taken to war. No doubt Livio's men had rushed here while Dandy had been busy with Theodora, and given the chaos that appeared to have taken place, Dandy could imagine the outrage of the stablemaster. But Dario was not here. Perhaps he'd gone to battle, too. Or if he'd kicked up enough of a fuss, perhaps someone like Lord Kerlin had killed him on the spot.

Euphy dragged him forward, calling out to the unicorn.

The great white head rose, slowly and heavily, but magnificent still, and Euphy let loose of Dandy's hand to fumble a set of keys out of his pocket, and jam the heaviest one into the lock.

But when it was open, he only hovered on the edge of the pen, clearly longing to throw himself forward and embrace the creature, but clearly not believing that he ought to. Though with how sluggish and sickly the unicorn looked, Dandy didn't think it would fight him even if he did. It looked as if whatever had happened between them had affected the unicorn as much as it had Euphy.

"Unlock his chains," Dandy urged, praying that Euphy wouldn't take his urgency for harshness, and that somehow, the minutes would lengthen. How could he repair everything he needed to when the riptide of battle was swiftly devouring their time?

Euphy's look grew pained anyway. "I don't have the key to those." His voice quavered. "I can't free him on my own. That was why I wanted to get close to Livio…or part of why…at first."

Of course. That was why Euphy hadn't just spirited the unicorn away from the start. Dandy had assumed it was because of the same misplaced obedience to Livio that Dandy himself had operated under for all these years.

"If you can't free him, you'll have to come back for him afterward."

"I won't leave him again," Euphy said, and Dandy knew from his hardened face that there was to be no convincing him this time, no accompaniment toward safety. This was how Euphy was going to regain himself. And just like before, Dandy knew that he could not force Euphy from it. It was only by being allowed to choose, to act as the person he wanted to be – the unicorn's friend and protector – that he could become that person once more.

Euphy, for his part, understood with perfect clarity now why Vanya had spent twenty years suffocating under the choice he'd made to abandon someone he'd loved. He would feel exactly the same if he were to leave Minari's side, if he had to live the rest of his life knowing that Minari's last moments were spent alone and deserted.

"I'll buy you as much time as I can out there," Dandy said.

"Can't you distract Livio first? Keep him from coming here? He doesn't have the power he wanted yet, but I'm sure he'll be here soon to claim it. He wouldn't go out to fight this battle without it."

"Whether he would or not, I'm not in Livio's service anymore. I doubt if I could get nearer to him than any of the rest of you."

198

"Then it really is the end. Of everything."

"Not everything," Dandy said, remembering Theodora's claim to distract Livio, but Euphy wasn't listening.

He was looking at the unicorn, eyes shining with tears, and he said in a choked voice, "If he were free, he could have taken on every one of them. If I had bothered to convince Livio to let him go instead of getting distracted with…"

"Euphy, you can't think about it now. Now you must protect him as best you can."

Then, to the creature who looked equally as despondent, "Unicorn, tell him. Heal him. Please, forgive him."

If Dandy had no more time to help repair Euphy, he knew he could depend on the unicorn to do it. Those eyes the color of sunlight on water would look into Euphy's heart and recognize what was needed to make it whole.

"Look forward, Euphy. Always forward. Your mistakes are not who you are," Dandy said. It was all he could give Euphy in these final moments – one lesson that his twenty years of folly had afforded him. He'd been so shaken to have to learn it, but he could see now that if he'd never done those things, or committed those crimes, he would not have had these words to offer to someone who didn't have the luxury of twenty years to learn it for himself.

He left the two figures, grief-stricken and silent as tombstone sculptures, willing them to hear more of his prayers than ever marble angel heard before, and dashed, sword in hand, to the tumult on Palomba Meadow for a second time.

CHAPTER 25
Mountain Spire

"Minari," Euphy whispered. "What are we going to do?"

He cast his glance around the stable, and his eyes fell on the wall where the farrier tools were kept – the rasps, the knives – all the tools that Euphy had used many times to set new shoes on horses, to bend the metal and nails into something more beneficial than they would have been on their own. He needed them now to turn Minari's bonds away from their original, hurtful purpose, though he carried them to the pen in full defiance of the fact he'd known since Minari first came to him – that chains which could hold a unicorn would never yield to such weak instruments.

And yet, he tried.

He sawed at the dark metal until his hands cramped with the effort, and the tools twisted and slipped from the sweat in his hands. They clattered to the floor and he finally cast himself onto Minari's neck with a sob.

"I could have freed you. I had the chance, if I hadn't gotten so caught up in what Livio could do for me that I forgot about what he could do for you. But Dandy was so cruel, and even now, I can't forgive him."

Euphy's voice broke on the last words. He felt that if he could summon up the fortitude to forgive Dandy, it might give him the right to ask for Minari's grace.

It might give him the strength to break these chains, even if it meant Minari would disappear into glory without him. But the sting of Dandy's words was deep, and all the more in that they had been a self-fulfilling prophecy – it was because he had been so hurt by what Dandy had said that Euphy had dreamed of allying with Livio in the first place.

But he could not find the strength to forgive Dandy any more than he could force himself to ask for it from Minari. He'd become just like Dandy and done those hurtful things to someone innocent, and he could not see that either of them deserved to be pardoned for it.

Dandy's fine and pretty words about moving forward sounded admirable, but how could Euphy do that when the one thing that mattered in the world was chained here with no means of moving at all, and all because of what Euphy had done?

"I don't expect you to forgive me, either" he got out finally. "But please just let me stay here with you until this ends. And if Vanya is the one who comes for you, I'd be glad if you'd remember me every now and then, when you go with him to his throne."

Minari shuddered beneath him, gingerly shaking his mane, and he lifted his head until Euphy sat up, face to face to with him.

In the Rainbow Hall, there had been a painting of the dale of Palomba, from the perspective of the nearby hills. It had looked so alien portrayed from such a distance, that Euphy didn't know how he could have lived and worked and spent his life in a place so foreign.

It was the same with Minari now. Minari, whom he'd cared for, who had trusted him, advised him, whose name he'd worked so hard to find, looked at him and Euphy felt as if he hardly knew him.

And then, the sunlight eyes flashed, and Euphy was no longer looking down to the depths of a valley. He was falling toward it, and the white mountain spire of a unicorn's horn was rising up to meet him.

There was no pain as it pierced him, only a flood of warm radiance filling his vision and his heart, forcing out the darkness of despair and regret.

He understood that Minari hadn't gored him in retaliation. He'd done it to heal him in a way that only a unicorn could.

Euphy didn't fall as the horn came away from him. It was the unicorn who went to the ground as Euphy breathed out in awe with lungs he was surprised still worked.

"So that's…" he started, but was interrupted by the sound of someone coming through the interior doors.

If he'd been in any sort of right mind during these past hours, he might have thought to barricade the doors, but it was too late for that now. And even in knowing that, the bite of self-reproach he would normally have felt didn't come; it had been taken away by Minari's cleansing horn.

From the doors, the voice of Livio called to him.

"You must cut it off," Minari whispered from his other side.

Euphy knew without asking what Minari meant; that it was not the chains he must try to sever now, and everything in him revolted at the thought

"I can't!"

"He does not know my name. The only other way to gain what he's seeking is by taking my horn. I will be of no use to him without it. If you truly wish to free me from him, you no longer have a choice."

Euphy's stomach turned as he looked at the discarded farrier's knife in the corner of the pen. But

Minari was right. All other options had been closed to them.

He darted to retrieve the knife. It was sharp enough to cut through a horse's hoof, and flesh and bone beside, if not handled with care. He hoped it would cut more than that now.

Euphy wrapped one hand around the horn, feeling the grooves running deep in the ivory, and set the knife at its base.

His first attempt was timid, but the horn was thick, and he soon found that nothing less than a rough sawing motion could make any difference on it.

As he worked, he realized that the beast was crying – great silver tears that splashed down and glittered on Euphy's lap.

Euphy's hands were wet with his own tears by the time he was done, and he fell back, clasping the treasure to him. His ragged breaths mixed with Minari's stifled whimpers, which were more terrible than his trumpeting that had threatened to shake the castle down.

And through all this, quiet and gentle, yet chilling Euphy to his core, was the voice he'd been used to hearing far above these dungeon walls, sighing, "Oh, Euphy. What have you done to my unicorn?"

CHAPTER 26
Penumbra

The field of battle was a perfect chess set in Bridle's mind, chaotic as it may have looked to any other observer. He could see himself in one corner, Golden in another, and Castan splitting the difference between them. He saw the other captains and their squadrons in constellated patterns across the expanse of green. And now, unexpectedly, he saw Dandy, cutting his way toward him from the opposite direction, atop the horse called Rusciu.

"You made it out!" Bridle shouted to him. "We didn't know *what* had happened to you with all of this going on."

"What about Castan?" Dandy pulled the horse up short next to him.

"He made it out, too," Bridle's face was joyful in between feints as he struck at two more of Livio's men. "What about Euphy?"

"He's with the unicorn."

"Did Livio really get its power?"

"Don't think so," Dandy said, cutting down a soldier who had tried to come between them.

"Probably the best place for Euphy, then. Unless it were here. Could use a helping hand."

Bridle wiped his brow with his sleeve. Being able to see the battlefield in all its array also meant seeing just where each side was struggling. The morris troops were executing their training perfectly, but the trouble came from the townspeople who had spontaneously joined their ranks since the hanging. Though sheer numbers did help, these people had no experience in battle drills, in listening for commands, or following them even if they did hear them. Most of them didn't even have any weapons, and were fighting with their bare hands.

Dandy also saw the issue, and while the civilians wouldn't be able to follow orders if he gave them, there *were* people on this battlefield who could. People who had followed his orders before.

Knowing Livio, it was possible that he hadn't bothered to inform the rank and file that Dandy had been cast off. The more people who knew the details, the more people who might question Livio's decision, and Livio hated that.

So if the soldiers didn't know, they might listen to Dandy. If he presented himself before them, and commanded them as if nothing had changed, he could intentionally misdirect them, give them orders that would play into the hands of the rebellion.

"There might be something I can do," he said to Bridle, who looked up at him with bright expectation, the way he'd done so many times before. If Dandy were to carry this plan through, this would likely be the last time Bridle would look at him that way.

If Dandy was successful in leading Livio's forces into defeat, there was the chance that he'd go into the grave with them. And even if he survived, he would have to explain just how he'd been able to make enemy soldiers listen to him.

"When you get inside the castle, there's a lady there; Theodora," he said, and Bridle caught the regretful tone even in the midst of the fight. "Don't hurt her. She's the rightful ruler now, the daughter of Nereus. You must help her to rule. Tell the others."

"The daughter of...? Wait, you mean – ?"

Dandy didn't hear him. He had already wheeled his horse around, and was soon gone from sight as he plunged into the thicket of advancing grey uniforms.

*   *   *

With one hand, Euphy reached for the knife which was covered in pearly dust. With the other, he clasped the horn as he rose to his feet.

"He's of no use to you now," he said, holding his terrible trophy before him for Livio to see.

Livio looked unnerved for a moment, but shook his head apologetically, as if he were sorry to say, "You understand that I'll have to take that from you, don't you?"

But Euphy still intended to keep his oath of protection. He wished that he'd retrieved the sword which remained in the hall where Dandy had knocked it from his hand. But a knife that would sever a horn from a unicorn was hateful enough, and perhaps that would suffice.

"It hurts me to see you do this," said Livio, having seen how Euphy's grip on the blade hilt tightened.

But Euphy was undeterred by the pained, pleading voice, However well it had fooled him before, it sounded false and hollow now compared to what he'd heard when...

"I want what's best for you; you know that, don't you?" Livio remonstrated as Euphy took a warning step forward. "I thought you agreed that the unicorn was safest in my hands, so that I could protect you, and everyone, from all of them." He gestured toward the outer doors, beyond which the noises of conflict sounded.

Euphy took another step. "He's not meant for anyone's hands, least of all yours."

He looked at Livio and thought of how this man didn't know what it was to form a real bond, to gain any real insight into someone's soul. All he knew was how to control, to take by force what he couldn't achieve through deception and had disdained to earn by compassion. That was why he had come in the night all those years ago. A knife in the dark was easier than looking your opponent in the face, and seeing them for who they were.

Livio's eyes dropped, and he did not speak for several moments. But then, his shoulders sagged, and he admitted, "I know that. I've always known it. I thought I could force it, but it was all for nothing in the end."

Euphy was fully prepared to ignore this show of humility. He had seen its like before, and none of it had been true. But in the words, he heard his own voice asking Minari for the same forgiveness. Euphy had also tried to force his own ends by walking a path in the dark, by betraying those he ought to have looked in the face and told the truth to. And hadn't he been granted absolution for it?

Was it possible that even Livio could be redeemed the same way? How could Euphy not try to show him? Knowing what it was to be redeemed from his mistakes, could he bear not to offer the same rescue to someone else? Even if Livio rejected it, Euphy had to try, for his own sake as much as Livio's.

"You've done so much wrong since you came to Ausonia. But I have, too." Euphy felt his breath catch as he turned to the white shape which had not moved since Livio's entrance, and he tried not to look at the empty space where the horn that was now in his hands used to be.

"If you beg his forgiveness, he might give it to you."

"Forgiveness?" Livio repeated. "Can it really be that easy?"

"It can be, if you mean it," said Euphy.

"But someone like me. Even if I mean it, how could he forgive me after everything that I've done?"

Euphy saw in Livio the same disbelieving desperation he'd felt before Dandy had walked with him to beg pardon at Minari's feet. Dandy – whom Euphy realized that he had forgiven, too. The hate that had consumed each thought of the man had disappeared along with the other dark shades which had taken up residence within him, and which Minari had replaced with weightless light.

"He forgave *me*, and that wasn't any small thing."

"Do you know, you're the first friend who ever cared enough to offer me such a thing?"

"Well, I know what it's like to need it." Euphy led Livio in kneeling before the motionless white head.

He leaned close over Minari's ear and whispered a plea for him to extend the same grace to Livio as he had to Euphy himself.

Livio, watching his example, also leaned forward. "There are so many things I need you to help me with, and that's why I'm asking you now," he started.

The next words Euphy heard were those of a man who expected not to be forgiven, but obeyed.

"Serve only me, Minari."

The sound of that name in Livio's mouth rolled as terribly as any of the sounds of the battle outside, and Euphy reeled back, trying to remember if he had ever actually told it to Livio amongst his other sins.

Was this where all of his efforts at redemption had gotten him? To a place where he still could not escape being used as Livio's puppet, not help but betray the one he loved most in the world?

Livio saw his confusion and laughed, not the gentle melody of the king in the Rainbow Hall, but a grating, writhing sound, the noise of a snake moving through dry grass.

"Haven't you guessed that there are more magicians in the world than yourself? Those who aren't given knowledge of a unicorn's mind can still enter it by force. It's especially easy when someone's done me the favor of stirring up its emotions. He was fighting me all the way until today, when he got distracted by fighting with you."

So that was the answer. Euphy had read of magicians with powers to penetrate into others' minds, but he hadn't known he'd had to fear that from Livio.

Beyond manipulating every human he thought could provide some point of access, Livio had been practicing spells of violation on the poor creature, like the dark wizards from the pages of *Fantastica*.

That would've been why Minari had grown so weak. To have to withstand such an assault, to deal with chains on his body and at the same time to be bombarded within his own thoughts, then to find that the one who had claimed to be his friend had been assisting in this attack; even a mind so proud and wild as Minari's would be hard-pressed not to fail under it.

He wished he'd had the same excuse for his own failures, but in the brightness which the unicorn had given him, he could now clearly see two things:

One: The forgiveness of the unicorn was complete. What he had done was in the past.

Two: Even if the unicorn had any power left to give, it could never be compelled to do anything by the name "Minari".

A voice that sounded like anything but Euphy's own thundered from his mouth, and he yanked Livio to his feet one-handed, as easily as if he were lifting a child.

"That is *not* his name," said the voice that sounded like gunpowder.

"What can you do to me, Euphemio? Now that I have your unicorn's power?" Livio asked with slithering laughter.

"You don't have his power. And what I can do is forgive you," Euphy answered as his hand twitched, and the spiral horn found a target for the second time.

CHAPTER 27
Whom I Will

"Wouldn't have expected the troops of someone called Ironhand to fight like that," Bridle huffed, wiping his face on his sleeve. "I'm not complaining, but I'd like to know what was going on. Why they acted like they *wanted* to be taken down."

"Uh-oh. Looks like there's someone you can ask," Emmanuel said, and Bridle whirled, fearing some fresh wave of attack to break the cautious hush which descended on the field like that of the morning after a storm.

Through the scenes of survivors picking their way through the aftermath came Vitalia and Diana, followed by a tall man from their squadron who was pulling Dandy along by bound hands, though Dandy appeared to be following willingly.

"What's all this?" Bridle asked. "You've picked up one of our own, you know."

"I know who he is," said tall Sterling as he forced Dandy to kneel. "But he was leading a troop of castle men. The only one of Livio's lords and commanders that was left. It's not hard to guess why, seeing as how he knew exactly what to expect from us. He wasn't caught on the back foot like the rest of them."

"You're confused," started Bridle, but his confidence faded when he saw that no one else – neither Vitalia, Diana, nor Dandy – was agreeing with him.

Dandy felt how simple it would be to say that Sterling had gotten it wrong, and that he'd had nothing to do with Livio in his life.

The old Dandy might have done it. But the old Dandy had done many things that weren't worth preserving.

"I did serve Livio once," he admitted. But since I've known you, I've thought of nothing but removing him from power."

"Is that what you were thinking of when you were fighting on his side just now?"

Dandy watched Bridle's face change into something hard and hurt, and angry. He thought of Euphy and how this wasn't the first time he'd let down someone who had trusted in him.

"It was. I'm sure you noticed how his forces played right into your hands. It was me who directed them that way. Who else would have known exactly the wrong place to be at every turn?"

"Then you just led your men straight to a slaughter? You didn't even let them have a fighting chance?"

The words chilled Dandy in spite of the heat of battle which still clung to him. Hadn't they all agreed that they were putting lives on the line when they'd entered the fray? Had he really done what Bridle had said?

"Didn't *you* want to defeat them?" he asked.

"I did, but not like that. Deceiving people, making them think you're on their side – it's too much like a Livian."

So then perhaps it wasn't possible to shed his old self. Maybe he could change his loyalties, but not his character. No matter what he did, he always wound up his power to hurt and destroy those weaker than him.

"You seem to be pretty good at deceiving people," Bridle reflected bitterly. "You fooled *us* well enough. I guess you would've learned it from your master."

214

"So was it you who turned me in?" Castan asked from beside him.

"It wasn't. I swear it."

"What good is it if you swear? If you would switch sides on them," he gestured to the unmoving shapes in grey uniforms that had once been Livio's soldiers, "How can we trust anything you're saying to us now? How can we know whose side you're *really* on, besides your own?"

"You can't," Dandy admitted, lowering his head. He'd known from the moment he'd left Bridle's side that it might be the last time they'd meet as friends. Up until today, he'd cherished the wish that everything he'd done to make up for the past would be enough, but he supposed it was better this way. It was cowardly to expect to escape the consequences of what he'd done, who he'd been for all these years. Whatever his former friends might decide to do to him, he would have to accept it as his just payment. A wrong so great must apparently be undone by an equally great punishment.

"I trust him," said a voice that Dandy didn't recognize. When the source of the voice appeared, if he had not already been on his knees, he might have sunk to them then. He hadn't believed the myth that ghosts walked on battlefields until this moment when an apparition in the form of Prince Vanya of Ausonia stood before him.

"Wasn't it you, Castan, who deemed him trustworthy in the first place?" said the figure, turning its eyes to the morrisman.

This shape that looked like the prince really must have been a ghost, thought Dandy, for how could he have known the details of how Dandy had joined the rebellion?

"I could have been lying to him," Dandy said. "Many people do. Livio does, and I was his man for years." He was unsure why he was arguing against his own favor like this, but he felt that he must confess all his sins, and

215

acknowledge how wretched a soul he was before the one he'd sinned against the most.

"Yes. I remember," said the ghost, and Dandy winced on seeing him raise a hand to the spot on his chest where Dandy's blade had once been.

"Then don't advocate for me," Dandy pleaded. "I don't deserve it. I don't expect to be pardoned by someone I've killed."

Vanya's eyelashes fluttered, as if he were startled out of a dream.

"You didn't kill me," he said.

"You said yourself that you remembered it. I've remembered it every day since then. My sword was in your chest."

"Oh, yes, and I felt it deeply. But I didn't die."

"You didn't…?" A ghost had been hard enough to take, but a resurrection from the dead was harder.

"If you can't believe me, put your hand here. Feel the mark you made, and how it has healed."

Dandy took off his glove, though he felt entirely unfit to touch this righteous apparition. To lay on this specter, or saint, or whatever he was, the very hand which had murdered him seemed as if it would burn Dandy, with all of his impurities, away on the spot. But he found he could not disobey the command.

Shaking fingers felt scar tissue knitted over the hole which had been pouring blood on a silver tunic the last time Dandy saw it, and felt the heart beating which had so stoutly faced the forces which had felled a king on a night which had been anything but glorious.

By laying his hand a second time on the prince of Ausonia, he, too, was being healed of the old wounds from that night. If the prince, who had the most right to condemn him could forgive all that Dandy had done, then Dandy's guilt would truly be erased. What he couldn't make up for by his own works would be redeemed by the prince's grace.

216

He felt himself falling forward, overcome, then felt Vanya's own hands supporting him. He looked up into the wise, kind face and asked, "How can I give you back what I stole?"

"You can't," Vanya said. There was no bitterness in the words. "But I wouldn't have you do so. The years that have passed, with both their good and their ill, are precious to me now. They've made me who I am, and there are many people who didn't get the chance to experience them at all. I don't begrudge what I went through to get here. Not anymore"

"How? How are you able to forgive so easily?"

"That's something the years gave me, too. If you had left me as I was, I might have been happier through them, but I wouldn't have learned nearly so much. I would've never learned how to stand on my own two feet, or to help others stand on theirs. So you see, your coming was turned to some good purpose, in the end."

Castan watched Vanya allowing Dandy to lean on him, speaking compassionately to him, and was reminded of a night in a town far away from here, when another man had needed a friendly face and a shoulder to lean on.

*　　　*　　　*

The cold rain was a balm after the fierce heat of the boxing ring. Castan stepped out into it, grateful for the icy drops that fell on the bruises he'd acquired at the hands of Gino Corrente. He could see steam rising from his skin where the water touched it, and counted it a blessing.

But he could also see that not everyone on this quickly-emptying street felt the same. Most people were ducking into doorways or raising what ragged cover they could find over their heads, which made the man who sat in the corner between the cutler's and the abandoned candlemaker's shops, making no attempt to shield himself from the cold or the rain, catch Castan's attention.

The man looked as if he'd come out on the losing end of one too many rounds in the ring. Castan had seen a good many lads who ought never have stepped foot into a boxing match trying their luck in one. He'd hated every time he was forced to pound their faces in for the entertainment of the cheering crowd, but everyone had to earn a living somehow.

If that was how this man had been trying to earn his, it was no great marvel that he'd been forced to beg on the streets. He looked so gaunt and sickly that even the greenest of boxers could probably knock him over with a touch.

Nonetheless, he didn't actually appear to be begging. He didn't sit hunched over the way beggars did, nor did he have his hands out for spare coins. Rather, he was sitting with unusually upright posture for one so frail, as if he didn't even notice the rain falling on his delicate form. In fact, he didn't appear to notice much of anything, for though his face was pointed toward the dirt path before him, his eyes were leagues away, seeing something from somewhere, or sometime, distant.

For a moment Castan was unsure whether the man was still breathing. It wouldn't be the first time he'd seen someone die with their eyes open in the street. Especially not since the false king had been on the throne, doing who-knew-what in his stolen castle while real Ausonians suffered in the grime and the dirt.

"What's wrong with you?" he ventured as he approached. Best not to ask whether the man were 'alright'. If he were alive to hear it, it would imply that Castan cared, and that might embolden the stranger to ask for a handout. But Castan had just come from having to earn his wages in blood. He was in no mood to give them to someone else for free.

218

The man's eyelashes fluttered, and it almost looked like he were working to pull his soul back into his body at the sound of Castan's voice.

He finally turned his gaze upward, and looked at Castan in wonder at being spoken to. His eyes were so very sad, but there was almost an innocence in them.

"Excuse me. What did you say?" He asked in an unsettlingly refined accent, not the rough tones Castan expected from a man in the gutter.

"I asked if anything was wrong with you."

"Oh...yes. Of course." His eyes were drifting back to that unknown, distant place as he said it.

"Are you sick?" Castan asked, knowing that he was going against his better judgement in asking it, but perplexed by the strange delicateness in this man. It felt like finding an expensive porcelain doll tossed into a garbage heap.

"I think I've been sick for a long time," said the man. "I don't know how to tell anymore."

"You don't know whether you're sick or not? What a bunch of nonsense. Surely you can tell if there's something the matter with you. If you make a habit of sitting in the cold and rain like this, I wouldn't be shocked if there were."

The beggar who was not a beggar sighed, a defeated sound, as if he'd been scolded that way before.

"I can't help it that there are so many things I don't know. I could tell you what I do know, but you wouldn't care to hear it about it. Not many people do."

He said it so quietly that Castan had to lean in to hear him. The soft voice, this elegant carriage, these tender eyes, they were not those of someone who had ended up here in the street because of his own choices. This was likely one of those many unfortunates who'd been stripped of everything because of Livio's cruel and careless regime.

"Started with Livio, no doubt. Just like the rest of us," Castan muttered, half to himself, but the distant eyes darted

toward him, seeming to perceive him more clearly than at any point prior, and Castan knew that his guess had hit the mark.

"Eh, go ahead and tell it," he said. Seeing this man's misfortune had set him in the mood to complain about the so-called ruler who had put them all in this condition.

"Are you certain? It's a very long story."

The rain which had been so welcome minutes ago was beginning to soak in, stiffening Castan's knuckles, which still throbbed from their contact with Gino Corrente's face.

If the weather were affecting him like this, hale as he was, then what must it be doing to the pale, listless form leaning against the wall?

Maybe it wouldn't be such a terrible thing to give away some of his money after all. Ignoring the suffering of others in favor of his own comfort was one of the very things Castan hated Livio for; how could it be right for Castan do the same?

"If it's going to take such a long time," he said, "then you can tell me somewhere where there's a roof and a drink to be had. I don't fancy listening to a long tale in this rain."

He looked around. "There's a public house right over there. Come with me and I'll listen to all you've got to say once we're inside."

The man's gaze dropped again, looking all the sadder for once having had a glimmer of life in it.

"I can't. I have no money. But thank you for the offer."

"Who said anything about money?" Castan demanded. "I've got enough for both of us."

*The fact that he **could** pay for someone other than himself – someone in need, whom Livio had trodden down – now seemed more a point of pride to be shared, rather than something to be jealously guarded.*

Besides, he'd spent so long beating others down, so long breaking them just to survive. If nothing else, it would be novel to build up someone who was already broken. And if he could counteract the harm Livio had done by helping just one person, then that small amount would be worth it. It would be more effective than silently cursing Livio with every swing he took in the ring, anyway.

"Come on, lad," Castan could hear his own voice going soft, but he brushed off the temptation to care about it, or to hide it with gruffness. "I'll take care of you for tonight. You'll have food and a room of your own, where you can be safe and dry until morning."

Hands that were swollen and bruised lifted up hands through which the edges of the bones showed through, and arms that were used to beating others down supported arms that could barely hold up their own weight.

As they walked, one leaning on the other, Castan pretended not to notice the difference between the tears and the raindrops rolling down this lonely urchin's face.

*　　　*　　　*

"Come on, General," Castan heard that once-lonely urchin saying, and saw the hands that had once required support from bruised and bloody ones now lifting up the bruised and bloody hands of another. The waif which Castan had met back then, who had found no welcome in an unforgiving world, was creating a world of forgiveness all his own.

On that first cold and rainy night, Castan had thought that if he could help even one person escape from the misery Livio had caused, then he would consider himself satisfied. In the end, by helping that one person, he had helped many more. By undoing the harm that Livio had done to Golden, he had undone Livio himself.

CHAPTER 28
Pietà

When the dungeon's great exterior doors were finally breached, sunlight and a force of twenty fighters poured in behind the prince, who found the king he had come for already twisted on the floor.

The white beast was on the ground not ten yards away, and his groom, whose hands were streaked with blood, was crumpled over him. None of them moved, and Vanya's first thought was that they had all killed each other.

He dropped to his knees, but when he touched Euphy's shoulder, a jagged sob tore the stillness, and Euphy lifted his head.

When he did, Vanya was not the only one in the room who gasped.

He could see that the unicorn's horn was now nothing more than a ragged stump, and Euphy was looking at him with eyes as vivid as sunlight on water.

"What's happened to…?" Vanya asked

At his question, Euphy dissolved into tears. It seemed that silvery eyes could cry the same as normal ones, and the sight of it was beautiful and awful to behold.

"He asked me to do it."

"Livio did?"

Euphy shook his head, and stroked the unicorn's mane.

"The unicorn asked you?"

"Livio was coming to claim his power, and I couldn't get the fetters unlocked," Euphy said. "There was no key, and I

223

wasn't strong enough to break them. He said that we could stop Livio if I took the horn first, but I think he's dying just the same."

He sobbed again, and the uncanny silver tears flowed as the sounds of his sorrow echoed off the stone walls.

Dandy, who stood with the group huddled around the open gate to the pen, was struck by how much the noise resembled the cries of the unicorn, whose voice had also once rung off the walls of this place.

As Vanya watched Euphy in this strange, otherworldly state, it struck him that this was what Livio would have become if he'd gotten the power he'd sought. Something supernatural, with eyes that would have flashed like lightning and a voice that would have thundered death and conquest more terrible than what he'd wrought twenty years ago.

But the unicorn had averted that calamity by giving its power to someone who was spending it on love and sorrow, who didn't seem to care, or even know what he'd been transformed into.

Vanya thought of himself, and how much he had cried the last time the throne had changed hands. There were always tears to be shed when it happened. But this time, he would not let any of the orphans of war face its aftermath alone. That was his job as king now: to ensure that no one else would suffer as he had.

He reached out to stroke Euphy's bent head, but his hand froze in midair when the beast slowly stirred, and sunlit eye met weeping sunlit eye.

"Do you truly think I am as fragile as that?" the voice asked, weak as embers. "As if I would die over such a trivial thing."

"I'm so sorry. I've hurt you so much." Euphy's words poured out frantically enough that Vanya didn't suspect how firmly they'd been stuck in Euphy's throat when the unicorn's horn had still belonged to its body.

"When I did – everything from before, and when I did *this* to you." He brushed his fingers over the remains of the horn as if afraid of breaking what was left there. "I've done a miserable job of acting like it, but I hope you can believe that I really did love you."

"What a foolish thing to have to ask," the creature responded. "It was because I already knew what was in your heart that I knew I could trust you. Do you think I would have given what I did to any human less worthy? Do you think anyone less worthy would have been able to receive it? Even Livio, who had me at his mercy all the time, still feared to try it until the end. You did not take anything from me; I gave it to you. All of it."

"But Livio knew...or he *thought* he did. Was he really invading your mind all of this time?"

The unicorn nodded.

"Why didn't you tell me?

"It wasn't as bad when you were near; I could withstand it then."

The distress in Euphy's face disappeared, replaced by a look Vanya realized he had seen on Castan's face many times, the first being on a cold rainy night on the street in front of a public house. It was the look of someone who does not at all mind being depended on.

"Then I guess the only solution is to never leave you again," Euphy said.

"You flatter yourself," replied the other, but he pressed his hornless forehead against Euphy's and made a sound that Vanya felt must have been a laugh, for it sounded like church bells ringing in the distance.

He was so awed by the sound that he didn't hear Euphy, whispering perhaps more quietly than ever human had before, except for those who knew the name of a unicorn, "Thank you, Luminario."

225

Meanwhile, from among the group of rebels which had crowded into the dungeon doors, someone elbowed his way forward to the open pen.

The morrismen looked and saw one of the townspeople who had spontaneously joined the attack on the gallows, but Euphy looked and saw the familiar face of Dario, though for the first time in all the years they'd known each other, Dario was the one to flinch back first.

"What's the matter? Why are you acting like you don't recognize me?" asked Euphy, noticing, finally, this new pattern in everyone since Luminario had pierced him – the wary looks they gave him when they first saw him.

Dario didn't answer. He looked to the prince for direction on what to say.

"Euphy, do you not know?" Seeing a water trough, he took Euphy by the hand and led him to look into it.

What stared back at them from the water was a man whose eyes shimmered like Minari's eyes, and how Euphy could have thought that his future would be anything but tied to the creature he loved felt like a distant dream to him now.

"So how do we get the chains off?"

From behind them, the quick and practical mind of Bridle had already accepted the novelty of the situation, and was eagerly working toward the resolution of the next problem.

"If you didn't have the key, do you know who did?" he asked Euphy.

"I don't know if there even was a key."

"If that's the case, we might find a mason somewhere who could file them off. Might take a while, but – begging your pardon," he addressed Luminario as he edged closer to inspect the fetters. "I do see a keyhole here. If Livio came to take the unicorn, I'd bet he brought the key with him."

Bridle took a breath, then fixed his face into resolute lines and knelt beside the corpse with a hole in its chest, which had left Euphy asking why the thing that had healed himself should have killed Livio.

"He wasn't willing to accept it," Luminario later told him. "You were seeking purification, and so received it. But purification kills that whose purpose is to fester and destroy."

"Ah, here we are," Bridle held up the key, his face brightening as he turned away from the dead king and placed the key into Euphy's hand.

"You do it. It's your honor," he said.

If this had been an illustration in *Fantastica*, Luminario would have risen majestically to his feet as soon as the chains fell away, with his head tossed high and his hooves drawing sparks from the ground – the way he'd done when he'd first arrived. But after everything that had happened, there was the proud but feeble failure of the creature to raise himself at all.

"Can you get up?" Euphy whispered to him.

"If you'll help me."

"I can't do it on my own. Will you be alright if the others help?"

The unicorn looked to the group appraisingly, and each person in the room felt themselves pass through a test which might have been much more trying had not Euphy spoken for them.

"You can trust them. I've learned that much," he said. Dandy, in particular, felt the weight of it when Euphy looked directly at him, and did not exclude him from this statement.

"If you trust them, then I do," said the creature, and Euphy turned to show person where to go, and what to do, to assist the unicorn.

Dandy did as he directed, and marvelled at how the beast who once would have gored or crushed him under its hooves now allowed itself to be helped and lifted up by his hand.

He knew it wasn't any form of meekness which allowed this. The animal was as regal and proud as ever, but he'd gained a tolerance born of love for Euphy and trust in his word.

When they had gotten the unicorn to its feet, many of them were left looking at their hands in disbelief, amazed that they could have touched a unicorn and lived.

Dario, though, didn't seem to have this problem. He was the first among them to find his voice, turning to the group of rebels alongside whom he'd already fought for life and death, but this didn't stop him from speaking to them like a disappointed parent.

"By the way, why didn't any of you tell me about this whole scheme beforehand? I would've been with you in a heartbeat." He put his hands on his hips, though his tone changed into something more reverent when faced Vanya.

"But look at you," he said. "You look like the king you were meant to be."

"Dario," Vanya dipped his head toward him "You've been loyal all this while. "

"Only twenty years. Not long at all," Dario answered, echoing his own words from that clear day when Euphy had first met both of them.

And as he had on that day, the prince smiled.

CHAPTER 29
Unicorn Sight

In the courtyard of Prisma Castle was a gathering which, though it lacked it pomp, was no less celebrated. This coronation was certainly more celebrated the previous one had been, but the new king had refused to ask the people so lately oppressed by Livio to pay for it.

"I'd say there's glamour enough with that one," said a woman in the crowd to her neighbor, inclining her head toward the shining white figure amongst the king's retinue, towering above the rest with a head held so high that none who saw it were in any doubt of what they were looking at, in spite of it not bearing the full horn that legend said it ought to.

"Were you really there when they freed him from the dungeon?" asked her companion.

"I was. I really touched him."

"Then do you know who that man with him is? And why he looks that way?"

Despite the size of the unicorn, they couldn't say that the man was standing in its shadow, for he seemed somehow to give off a little light of his own. Even his eyes seemed to reflect the sunlight unusually brightly.

Nor were these spectators alone in noticing him. Those who had worked with him in the castle marvelled that the humble horse's groom they'd known was now part of a coronation procession, though an intelligent-looking librarian declared herself unastonished.

"You see what studying does for you. He was a stablehand before he started coming to the library, and now he's up there with the new king."

"He looks like a fairy knight," said the friend who stood next to her.

"Yes, well, he did read a lot about fantastical creatures, now that I think about it."

Others speculated that this seeming fairy knight and his unicorn had brought the prince back after so many years, though some whispered that the big, stern man who had stood next to Vanya, and who had once stood on the gallows, was responsible for that.

"He's a magician. A necromancer," one of the more superstitious among them said.

"If he's that powerful," came the argument from the believer's companion, "then why didn't he rescue himself from the gallows? Why did he need the prince to do it?"

"That's *how* he brought the prince back. To summon the spirits of the lost and the dead, you have to tread on the borders of death yourself."

"And the princess, too?"

They looked at another figure who had stepped out from the mists of the New Glory's misery. Alongside the necromancer and his resurrected prince, the shining unicorn, and the transfigured stablehand stood a woman with sharp eyes that were very like in shape to the eyes of the king.

"She wasn't summoned because she didn't die. You see the man with her? He was loyal to King Nereus since the old days, and he's kept her safe and hidden away all this time, but he pretended to be loyal to Livio, so that he wouldn't be suspected."

With this dubious information thus shared between two spectators, the ceremony began with Dandy, as the last official representative of Livio's reign, declaring his recognition of Vanya's victory, and of his right to rule.

That had been Bridle's suggestion.

"In case anyone tries to claim that Golden stole it from Livio, instead of the other way around," he'd said. "They can't argue if the Morningstar says it."

"And let them visit his portrait in the Gallery if they doubt his authority," Theodora had added proudly, taking Dandy's hand.

He was surprised that she sounded so pleased about something that had been his shame for so many years.

"You see?" asked Vanya, reading Dandy's thoughts. "Your time with Livio has come to some good purpose in the end. No one but you could fill that role for us now."

After Dandy's part in the ceremony, came a party of citizens gathered from across the country. Some were less nervous than others, and least of all a woman with a scarf tied around her head, who led them with a steady gait, and gave her answers evenly and clearly when Emmanuel, acting as officiant, asked these representatives of their regions whether they accepted Vanya as their king. And to her credit, she only flinched slightly when she had to pass by the unicorn on her way back to her place.

231

The crowd went breathlessly attentive as Luminario stepped forward next, his hooves ringing like metal on the ground as Euphy walked beside him, until they were both facing Vanya.

Emmanuel, with his grave tones and dignified bearing, asked "Do you, unicorn, who are tied to our land of Ausonia with a deep and ancient bond, give Vanya, the son of Nereus, your blessing as rightful ruler of this kingdom?"

"I do."

"And have you bestowed such a blessing on any other person claiming to be king in this castle before?"

"I have not."

Luminario tossed his head, though he knew that Euphy had asked for this question to be included, so that everyone who had read Castan's execution announcement would be undeceived by the lie Livio had written there.

Emmanuel turned to Vanya, asking him if he would commit to serve and protect Ausonia and all of its inhabitants, and to rule with justice, truth, and kindness.

All of this Vanya swore to do, after which Emmanuel raised Vanya's crown – not the crown of Nereus which Livio had claimed for his own, but a new work, created by the artisans of Clockface, with the jewels of the old had placed in a new, simpler setting.

"Then by these five confirmations: the concession of the prior government, the endorsement of the people, the blessing of the unicorn, his hereditary right, and his own solemn oath – Ausonia declares Vanya of the House of Nereus its king."

With the crown and the title placed on him, Vanya kneeled, and all those beside him followed, facing the crowd to symbolize their dedication to serving the people and to bringing them into the dawn following the long Night.

When they stood, Euphy looked to Vanya on the other side of Luminario. The thought of this moment, when the prince and the unicorn would stand next to each other amidst celebration and ceremony had placed a wedge between him and all he'd loved, and driven him to jealousy, despair, and darkness. But now, seeing it happen in the light of day, he could think of nothing more beautiful.

*   *   *

The cheering of the crowd was repeated months later at the marriage of Princess Theodora and Dandy the Morningstar. It was said among the people that it was a political marriage meant to cement the goodwill between the old reign and the new, though those who observed them also said that they had never seen an arranged bride and groom so happy in the match.

And there were many who had their chance to observe them, as the pair could be found in the towns as often as in the castle, serving as patrons of the communities, and lives, being rebuilt after the negligence of Livio.

Of Theodora, they noted how unflaggingly interested she was in everything she saw, as if she were encountering it for the first time. But even in this, she wasn't naïve. When she spoke her opinions, it was with confidence and conviction, though without arrogance.

Of Dandy, they noted how pleased he was to hear

the feelings and opinions of each person he spoke to. He listened to them with such thoughtful attention that they felt they were the most important person he'd ever met. His ideas were as strong as Theodora's but he only formed them after considering everyone else's views on the subject at hand.

Their visits were always anticipated by the townspeople, but they weren't the only members of Vanya's court whom people were often eager to see. Many were interested in seeing the man with the light eyes who, though he often looked serious and righteous, smiled just as easily.

He was called handsome, but to Euphy's eyes, it was all the others whose beauty presented itself every day. Every face he saw carried on it the tapestry of a life, woven by the marks that life had left on it.

How dazzling were the lines of care that Vanya's face had gained since he'd been that prince of yesterday, for each one spoke of experience and wisdom gained from the year that formed it. How beautiful was the way the youthful softness of Bridle's mouth had transformed into a firmer, more refined line, though it was no less cheerful for all that, and his laughter was often heard ringing in a bright duet with that of the king, whose laugh ran like water through Prisma's halls, washing clean every dark corner where haunted memories had settled in the years when that laugh had gone silent.

"Castan, didn't anyone tell you?" Bridle was saying as they all stood in the old Gallery of Battles, where most of the paintings had been removed except for *The Night of New Glory*, showing the death of Nereus, beside which a new work titled *The Resurrection of Vanya the Golden* had been hung.

"We were supposed to pose for a battle scene, not the most eligible bachelor competition. Is that how you looked when you went to the seaside?" Bridle struck an exaggerated imitation of Castan's expression in the image.

"Look, if all you're going to do is criticize, you can keep it yourself," Castan said.

"Please don't be angry." Bridle recognized the old familiar habits coming back, and he truly wished to never have to fight with Castan again, because as the painting showed, fighting together was so much better.

"You look good. Seriously."

Castan could see Golden, behind Bridle, working to stifle his own smile in an attempt to help Bridle keep the peace, and his anger faded at the sight. How could he stay angry when this was the very thing he'd wished for: the lost prince restored to his rightful place, and happy? Or how could he forget the look of joy on Bridle's face when they'd found each other on the battlefield, and what he'd later learned from Golden about how Bridle had cried over him all night?

In the which silence settled over them – one distinctly lacking the tension which used to follow their disagreements – a plea could be heard from he other side of Theodora, who stood looking at the two paintings.

"Oh, ma'am. Have them take the first one down. Sell it to Albion or somewhere," her fidgeting maid implored her.

"They don't want it," Dandy answered. "The reason he came here in the first place was because he'd

235

already made some attempts at power there, and he'd made enemies because of it, too."

"Weren't you afraid they'd see you as an enemy, too, when you went back to tell them what happened, sir?"

"They were his enemies before I met him. They didn't mind me because I was someone who helped him get out of Albion, which meant I took him away from them."

"So that's why they weren't upset when they heard about how he passed," Marta said, lifting her eyes to the new painting.

"I wouldn't sell it to them even if they wanted it," Theodora put in. "These two are part of the same story. If you forget what happened in the first half, you can't really know where you are now."

"She's right," Vanya added. "How can you fully appreciate who this is," he motioned to the victorious image of himself in the *Resurrection*, then toward the bent and bleeding prince of the *New Glory*, "without knowing that this is who he was? How can you understand the importance of these," he pointed to the likenesses of all those who had fought beside him, "without knowing what they had to go through to get here?"

Marta, not as used to Vanya as she was to Dandy, backed behind Theodora with her head lowered.

"Forgive me for questioning it, sir."

"There's nothing to forgive. You have no need to apologize simply for how you feel. I welcome hearing the concerns of everyone."

He knew how it felt to have someone take the time to care about his own sorrows – from the first time Castan had held out a hand to him, through to the days when Euphy had listened to all the things he couldn't even tell Castan – and how those moments of sympathy had changed his whole fate.

"Even serving maids?" asked Marta meekly.

"Even serving maids. And shepherds and stablehands. Or street boxers," he said, looking around at the others. "There is not one person whose troubles I wouldn't gladly help bear."

"Then, sir, I do have one more thing I'd like to ask. Why do they call you call you 'Golden?'"

The unicorn raised its head from Euphy's shoulder, and the peal of its voice made Marta jump.

"That is what his name means. I used to hear the wood elves call anything golden and beautiful by that name, long ago."

"Father always said that was why they named him so," Theodora affirmed.

"So that was what she couldn't recall," Dandy muttered to himself. "But it came to some good purpose in the end." It had pained him at the time, but if Theodora hadn't once forgotten this ancient meaning of her brother's name, Dandy would never have gone to the library to search it out, and he never would have met Euphy or the morrismen, whose mission had been the saving of him.

Golden and beautiful, indeed.

CHAPTER 30
Fantastica Nova

"Is it here yet?" Euphy stood before the librarian's desk, his excitement a marked difference from the apprehension of the man who had approached her desk, trailing behind General Morning months ago.

But they'd all gone through changes since then, she reflected.

"It's right here. I told you I'd send for you when it was ready, didn't I? Though I can't say I blame you for checking so often. I'd probably do the same if it were me."

She handed him a volume bound in new blue leather, with *RESEARCH IN FANTASTICA* imprinted with fresh gilding on the cover.

"You get to be the first reader of the new edition."

"I'll make sure to have it back on time."

"You don't have to; that one's yours. We have another copy for general circulation."

"Really? I already have the older one. I get to keep this one, too?"

"I think you deserve it, considering the circumstances. Go on and see what it says."

Euphy flipped through the crisp, clean pages to the section whose every word he knew by heart, until among the familiar text he found a passage that had formerly ended with only a short footnote. It was expanded now with words he was reading for the first time, though he knew the subject well enough:

"*When treated with kindness, a unicorn will grow so gentle that even young maidens may direct it. But when treated with cruelty, it will become so savage that even a king cannot withstand its onslaught. Those who come in contact with a unicorn must be careful in which direction they turn its fire.*

Coppelia of Jonani is one of the most well-known examples of a human drawing forth the tenderness of a unicorn, and most representations of one with its head resting in a maiden's lap are derived from the account given in Carletto's **Rare Beasts of the Wild***.*

In more recent times, Euphemio Benedetti of Prisma Castle has been observed as one who has fully illustrated the two sides of the creatures' nature. The same unicorn whose horn was used to kill King Livio the Ironhand (who had usurped the throne of Ausonia in the year 1504), is known to be so dedicated to Euphemio that the two are rarely seen apart, and the animal is commonly known as 'Euphy's Unicorn' among the circles of King Vanya's court. (Vanya being the rightful king whom Euphemio and the unicorn assisted in reclaiming the throne in the year 1524.)

Given that Euphemio's first and surnames together signify 'Fairword the Blessed' in Old High Ausonian, it is fitting that he should have come into this destiny. By speaking words of kindness to the unicorn, and treating it with love instead of seeking to dominate it as Livio had once done, he has received this rare blessing."

"It makes you sound like some grand lord," said the librarian when she looked up from the page in her circulation copy.

"All the times you were in here quiet as a mouse, and I never guessed you were doing great things elsewhere."

"Well, I did some things that weren't so great, too."

"But you turned it around, didn't you? According to this," she flipped through her pages, "the unicorn wouldn't stick so close to you if he were angry about whatever you'd done. He must have forgiven you, or all this about the two of you wouldn't be in here."

"I had to beg him to do it."

"But you did ask. That sounds like a grand thing to me."

"In that case, can you forgive the fine on *The Glass Castle* from last week? I swear I'm still looking for it, but it's hard to keep track of things like that in the middle of so many other grand and important things, you know."

His short bout of regret had vanished, replaced by a cheeky grin.

"Get out," she swatted at him, laughing.

Still smiling, Euphy tucked his gleaming new copy of *Research in Fantastica* under his arm, and when he reached his chambers, he set it on his shelf next to the old, battered copy he'd first known. He looked at them, and loved them both. The first was beautiful with all of its scratches and wear, because every moment which had battered was a moment in which Euphy was learning to find his way.

The second was beautiful because it took those moments of experience and built a new tale out of them. On the foundation of the old stories were new, fantastical ones to be lived, in this book of shining letters on a field of unmarred blue.